WREATH OF HONESTY

Wreath of Honesty

PAT BURDEN

A CRIME CLUB BOOK
DOUBLEDAY
New York   London   Toronto   Sydney   Auckland

A Crime Club Book
Published by Doubleday
a division of Bantam Doubleday Dell Publishing Group, Inc.
666 Fifth Avenue, New York, New York 10103

DOUBLEDAY and the portrayal of a man
with a gun are trademarks of Doubleday,
a division of Bantam Doubleday Dell
Publishing Group, Inc.

Library of Congress Cataloging-in-Publication Data

Burden, Pat.
Wreath of honesty / Pat Burden. — 1st ed.
    p. cm.
"A Crime Club book."
I. Title.
PR6052.U614W74   1991
823'.914—dc20   90-19586
CIP

ISBN 0-385-41863-9
Copyright © 1990 by Pat Burden
All Rights Reserved
Printed in the United States of America
June 1991
First Edition in the United States of America

10 9 8 7 6 5 4 3 2 1

WREATH OF HONESTY

ONE

Bassett—ex-Detective Chief Superintendent Henry Bassett, to give him his full title—was on hands and knees in his cosy country kitchen being playfully attacked by his pup. The fighting and chasing switched suddenly to a drag-the-Bassett-round-by-the-sleeve game, and between them they were making so much noise, were so absorbed in their fun, that neither of them heard the click of the front gate or the footsteps on the path. Only as the door began opening did Bassett realize he had a visitor. With a quick command to pup and a clumsy kind of haste he hauled himself to his feet.

"What do you look like, Mr. B!"

Bassett glanced down at himself: at the cardigan riddled with pulled stitches, one sleeve miles longer than the other; at the big toe peeping out of a chewed slipper; at the trouser bottoms frayed—and said disarmingly, "I've been puppied, Sally!"

"Honestly . . . !" Plump and jolly widowed pensioner Sally, who cleaned and polished for Bassett two mornings a week, issued this further gentle reprimand and chuckled. "That pup'll be the death of you! . . . Won't you, precious?" she said, stooping down to receive a lick and give a cuddle. For even she, who had brought up a large family in a two-up two-down farm cottage and had been forced to say no to all when pets threatened to become too numerous, couldn't resist Bassett's adorable six-month-old labrador. "Come here, let's have a feel o' them velvety ears."

Bassett surreptitiously checked the kitchen calendar. Tuesdays and Fridays were Sally's days; he usually straightened round before the good lady came, donned his second-best, and made a point of having a shave; a sort of courtesy gesture. Sally thought he was ever such a tidy person.

"It's all right, Mr. B," came her voice from ground level. "It is only Thursday."

"Ah!" Caught again! Her senses were as keen as his some-times, she missed nothing. Bassett self-consciously rubbed his nose with a knuckle. "Thought I'd lost a day."

"No. There, there," Sally said indulgently. "You go and play now." She shooed pup onto the sunny porch, watched the little dog spring from step to garden, and up to the front gate; returned her attention to Bassett.

"I'm not due till tomorrow, but I baked a cake for you." She took a parcel from her basket and placed it on the table. "Date and walnut," she said, tapping it with a finger. "Ages since I made you one of these."

"You're very kind, Sally." Bassett smiled. She smiled back. "Makes up for the eggs and things you give me." He flicked an eyebrow. "I was just going to make a cuppa," he fibbed. "Fancy one?"

Sally thanked him, but no. "Julie's waiting for me in the van." Her oldest son's girl, come to spend a day with her gran. "I'm going to show her the bluebells. But must drop in on Mr. B, I told her, Detective Chief Superintendent Bassett as was."

Bassett grinned: sounded as if he'd changed his name when he married. Or retired. Sally said it to tease; and she didn't always get it right. "I was telling Julie how you're a countryman now," she went on chattily.

"Trying to be, eh, Sally?"

"Well, yes, I did say you didn't think you'd ever be a proper one. You kept pigs but wouldn't eat them, felt guilty taking the hens' eggs, and fed pheasants and wild rabbits in winter, but wouldn't bag one for the pot."

"Told her I'm bringing pup up the same?" Bassett said whimsically.

"Matter of fact I did, yes! Funny, that little dog is, I said. All she does when she sees a rabbit is wag her tail!"

They both laughed. Bassett winked. "Like some eggs for Julie to take home with her?"

"Well . . . ." Sally's homely face flushed with pleasure. "It's not why I came." Yet she *was* hovering.

"Hang on—"

"Mr. B—?" Bassett detected a sudden seriousness in her voice. He waited, but, "Nothing," she said; and it was gone. He continued to the pantry.

"Saw Tod Arkwright sneaking down the back lanes!" She was speaking chattily once more.

"Sneaking?" Bassett said over his shoulder.

"What it looked like. Although he was a-singing," she added perkily. "What he calls singing, anyway. Ever heard him? Honks, he does; down his nose, like. Don't tell him I said so, though." She laughed. "He probably thinks he sounds like Caruso . . . On his way to Crum Cottage for rhubarb."

Crum Cottage. Bassett didn't recognize the name. He brought out the eggs, a baker's dozen. "There," he said, "still warm . . . And you know, Sally, if ever you have a problem, and I can help . . ."

She studied his face while he packed eggs into her basket. A nice face. Like his canine namesake, was how Mary Bassett had once endearingly described him. A soft-jowled mournful face with expressive eyes he could produce on cue. He was wearing that same expression now; as if he cared . . . But there was a right way and a wrong way to go about things; you couldn't just blurt them out . . . Tomorrow. Tomorrow she would be better prepared.

"Will you be in tomorrow when I come, Mr. B?"

"I'll be in," he said perceptively.

"Perhaps we could talk about it then, if you wouldn't mind." She made a face, laughed, bustled. "I'd best move myself. Julie'll wonder where I am!"

She dashed off; and Bassett remembered too late that he could have given her a bunch of lilac to go with the eggs. He went upstairs to change.

Outside in the lane Julie opened the van door for her grandmother. "What did he say?" she asked eagerly.

"I didn't ask him."

"Oh, Gran . . ." Julie chided.

"Don't rush me," Sally scolded the girl. "He knows I want to talk to him about something, that's a start—"

"You said he's nice—"

"He is. But he's retired and we mustn't impose. Anyway, things might be done differently now from in his day."

"Oh, Gran," Julie scoffed gently. "He solved that murder last year, didn't he? Meaning he must still be *in* with the police—"

"All the same, tomorrow I said and tomorrow it'll be. Come on, now! Lovely day like this! Mustn't waste it!"

It was indeed a lovely day. An early spring had followed a mild winter. It was now May and everywhere was green and fresh and alive. Bluebells seemed bluer than ever; hedges were filled with white blossom; meadows with buttercup yellow; and birds sang profusely. A gorgeous day. If proof were needed—look at Tod! Tod Arkwright, retired estate-worker and local gloom-and-doom merchant: the only man Bassett knew who could be doubled up with laughter and still look a picture of misery. Today Tod was smiling. And for Tod to smile, and for the smile to show . . .

This was the selfsame Tod Sally had referred to. If he appeared to be sneaking—well, he had his reasons; if he was sticking to back lanes, there was method in that madness too: he preferred to enter Crum's garden from the rear. Almost there. This stretch backed on to Bassett's semi-wild bottom garden. Mud up to your armpits on this track in winter, rutted but dry now, thank goodness. He ceased the singing that Sally called honking, picked his way across the track and up to Bassett's hedge. An ancient hedge, thin in places. At one of these gaps he peered through: at Bassett and a cluster of hens.

It was common knowledge now in the sprawling village of Oakleigh how Bassett and his wife Mary had fallen in love with this area of unspoilt countryside where the counties of Herefordshire, Worcestershire, and Gloucestershire meet, and how lucky they considered themselves when they acquired Keeper's

Cottage, a retirement haven. Its very name bespoke a situation surrounded by ancient woodland. Well known also, since little seemed to have changed here in decades, was Mary's fear that she and Bassett might be regarded as intruders. But bless you, no! they were such friendly souls—"No side on 'em"—that in no time at all they were accepted members of the community.

Tod and others had thought that Bassett might return to old haunts when Mary died a year later, but he liked it here, Bassett said, he liked the people, the wildlife.

"Ar, he's in his element," Tod muttered to himself.

Tod called now through a gap in the hedge. "Where are you, then?" Grand little dog, he told everyone; as if the country wasn't rich with dogs. Champion. Bassett's salvation when Mary got took.

It was actually Tod himself, Jack the Poacher, Jessie and other village friends who had been Bassett's immediate salvation, but Tod wasn't to know that. Pup had arrived later, after Bassett had decided to stay.

Bassett looked, located and answered the voice. "Beautiful day, Tod! Can't pick her up now, too heavy!" During the winter he'd carried pup everywhere tucked inside his belted jacket; a few weeks ago he could have carried her down to Tod; alas, no longer. "I've some cold ale, if you're interested!"

Tod was interested; but, "Going to Crum Cottage for some rhubarb," he called. "And I'd best get a-pulling it afore this sun gets too far up. So I'll see you on the way back!" His voice rose up and over a thick may hedge as he moved on. Somewhere, the sound carrying on the air, a woodpecker drilled. Bassett smiled, turned, ambled slowly back up the slope towards the opened french windows.

He didn't go in. He watched hens revelling in dust baths among his young lettuces and carrots, bullfinches pinching the fruit buds off his cherry tree, pup lolloping after a butterfly across his once immaculate lawn . . . Moles be rascally this year! someone had said the other day. Rascally! Bassett's orchard resembled the aftermath of the Battle of the Somme! And his chimneys were blocked. Again. Like the Berlin Airlift some mornings, jackdaws flying in with nesting material. He wondered if he ought to feel put upon.

It was then, when his eyes lighted on his own rhubarb, practically the only thing in his garden that pets and wildlife allowed him to have all to himself—no matter that he never ate the stuff!—that the copper in him surfaced.

He asked himself why Tod, a countryman all his life and owner of a garden as big as this one, found it necessary to gather rhubarb from somebody else's patch. Surely the old gamekeeper had some of his own?

Crum Cottage. Crum Cottage . . . He tapped his memory box. Yes. Yes, of course he knew it! Half a mile down the lane. Empty. At least, the last time he'd looked there had been nobody living in it.

The slight emphasis on the "living" was in no way deliberate.

TWO

Crum Cottage, tucked snugly behind a low wall and creepers in a crease of a hill, was often overlooked. Ask for certain directions when at the top high end of the lane in which Bassett lived, and most folk would say "Down past Hillside Cottage, past Keeper's, and you'll come to Foxgloves . . . the road narrows there between sandstone, you'll likely wonder where you're at, but keep going and you'll see . . ." and quite forget Crum Cottage somewhere in the middle.

Yet when you did look at it properly you would see it was a pretty little place, in good repair. Its windows were sturdy and shut tight; the roof was good. The cottage had been painted white, and its curtains—what you could see of them—were lined and revealed no tell-tale stains of neglect or even fading.

To a passer-by the cottage might have seemed lived in: by someone desirous of privacy. But in three years Bassett had seen no sign of life; never a wisp of smoke from a chimney; and in winter only fox and bird prints in the snow by the gate and on the path to the garage . . . Who owned it? Mary Bassett had once inquired. A distant relative of the previous owner, she had been told, the old lady left him the cottage when she died. He's a musician, said one. A missionary, said another. No one really knew; but absentee landlords were invariably something out of the ordinary, something special. Only Tod had ever met the man, a year or two before the Bassetts moved to Oakleigh, and then not actually to talk to him, merely to pass the time of day.

Tod had, in truth, taken advantage of a chance meeting, had sought and received permission to gather rhubarb, and had made one, occasionally two visits a year for that purpose ever since.

Funny old stick though, Tod. Despite the consent, he felt uncomfortably like a thief when he was helping himself. And so he acted like a thief. This was why he appeared to sneak, to hug the back lanes, and why now and then he was agitated. Yet conversely, as if subconsciously to ward off accusing fingers from pointing, he made no secret of his destination: he sang, and he told. "Going to Crum Cottage for rhubarb."

Once inside the back garden—there was not much more than an overgrown herbaceous border at the front—the old gamekeeper would honk his loudest, kick a rusting forcing bucket or two, and generally make a din so as to announce his presence, in case anyone was at home. The feeling that he was trespassing usually prevented him from going right up to the cottage. Only twice in five years had he done so: the same year that he met the new owner, and two years ago amid rumours of antique thieves on the prowl, when he had taken young Davey Mellor along to check doors and windows.

Today was to be another exception. The old eyes were drawn repeatedly to a splash of crimson, brilliant against the white wall of the cottage, where it was caught by the sun. As he applied string to his first bundle of rhubarb he looked again; again something nudged him inside his head. This time he acknowledged the nudge. Dabbing sweat from the back of his neck with a none-too-clean handkerchief, he narrowed his eyes to see minutely . . . Was it . . . ?

No awkwardness now as he approached the cottage. He had only one purpose in mind. *Was* it what he thought . . . ? He beamed. It was, you know! Ar, it was an' all! Never seen any a-growing here afore. Must've knowed he were a-looking for some—!

He reached where the honesty plant had taken root in among broken paving stones by the door, and bent down for a closer look. He smelt something. Sniffed, and reared his head. Sniffed. And sniffed again.

The smell was indistinct. Elusive.

Bad.

Coming from where? The old nose, pitted and red, twitched, moved this way and that, up in the air and down; drew Tod away from the honesty flowers to the drains, the dustbin, the coalshed, the ground immediately around Crum Cottage—all comparatively sweet—and back to the door.

Dry rot? In the door itself? Once more the nose moved, and twitched, like one of his ferrets scenting prey. It wasn't a dry rot odour. Besides, the door was good. Firm. Secure. Rodent-proofed at the bottom. A solid old-fashioned door, built when wood was wood, and door keys weighed a ton.

Gingerly Tod put his nose to the gap between door and jamb . . . sniffed . . . and backed off. His face took on both a puzzled and a faintly horror-stricken expression. He had tried the door that day he came with young Davey. Was it still locked? Something told him it was not. With a feeling of presentiment he wrapped a hairy-knuckled hand round the brass door knob . . .

Within seconds he was outside again, gulping fresh air and clutching at his insides to stop himself from retching.

A few minutes later he was crashing through Bassett's bottom hedge. "There's a dead'un a-sitting in old Mother Crum's place, Harry! Long time dead."

THREE

A narrow entrance hall with a red quarry-tiled floor and cream-painted walls. On the right, a kitchen and walk-in larder. On the left, a few paces on, the open doorway to a semi-furnished sitting-room. Here Bassett halted and viewed the body. It was the body of a fully-clothed man who sat facing him in a high-backed fireside chair. He studied corpse and room for a while, then put away his handkerchief: worse sights than this had confronted him in his day.

He called to Tod hovering by the back step, "Touch anything, Tod?"

Only the door to the sitting-room. It had been ajar, Tod had pushed it further open with the toe of a boot.

"What about the curtains?"

"I seen all I wanted without touching curtains!"

Bassett ran his eyes round the room once more. Beige carpet, what Mary would have called a mixture. A smaller chair on this side of the fireplace, its back half-turned towards him. A gas heater on the hearth. A big comfortable-looking settee in the centre of the room, with a low mahogany table. The far wall was fitted with shelves and corner cupboard, shelves empty. The long wall on his left, facing onto the lane, carried two windows about six feet apart.

"Sure you didn't touch the curtains—?"

"Harry," Tod replied lugubriously, "where you are a-standing is as far as I got."

Bassett nodded. Using a ballpoint from his pocket, he tried the light switch. No power on.

"Any idea who he might be, Tod?"

"Mebbe a tramp."

Not these days. Bassett crooked a finger, went into the room, Tod with some reluctance moving up to the doorway; but no further.

"No tramp," Bassett observed. "Not in these clothes." For the dead man was wearing a suit with waistcoat fashioned from good quality suiting, a silk tie, Crombie overcoat, expensive, possibly handmade shoes, and leather gloves. Even in death, even in this condition, the body retained ironically the air of a successful man.

"Mebbe the owner then, come a-visiting and got took bad. Could've been here all winter, poor bloke . . . Dunno his name," Tod rumbled, replying to Bassett's next question. "I seen him just the once five years back."

"Think this is him?"

"Could be. Could be anybody, couldn't he?" The eyes Tod gave Bassett were pained. He wasn't looking at the body, might not have looked properly at the body at all: one glance and an overall impression would have been enough.

"Tod—" Bassett began. But could he really insist on the already shaken old gamekeeper coming closer? He altered his tone of voice, made it brisk, matter-of-fact, and added a smile to lift any stress there might have been on death and decay. "Say late forties, well built, six feet or thereabouts, plenty of hair turning grey—"

"No-o. 'Twas a youngish man I met. Thirty-five mebbe."

"Five years ago, though . . . ?"

"Ar, you're right. He were tanned then. Healthy-looking. Just back from foreign parts. But ar"—Tod wagged his head thoughtfully—"he were a-buzzing off again for a few years, summat-a-that. So mebbe this *is* him come home. Snuffing-it's bound to age a man."

Whether this last was an attempt at levity, or simply a statement, at any rate speculation, uttered Tod Arkwright fashion, Bassett couldn't tell.

"Mebbe he's a-carrying a wallet. Or passport—"

Ar, mebbe he is, Bassett thought. He forbore to touch the
body, however. "Best leave it to the police, I think. Let's go see
the kitchen."

The kitchen had been modernized many moons ago. It had
an enamelled sink with draining-board, fitted cupboards and
dresser, bulky post-war fridge. No door to the room, but hooks
for a bead curtain. Sunshine flooded in via the entrance hall
and through a far-higher-than-average window hung with net
curtains . . . A faint haze of neglect on blue and cream sur-
faces, insect debris and cobwebs here and there but no in-
grained dirt—this and the key on a large table Bassett had
noted on his way in. Now he directed his old friend's gaze.

"Tod—that key. Don't touch it, but would you care to go and
see if you think it's the one for the door."

"It'll be the one," was the swift reply. "I seen it afore. Used to
come here regular when Tabitha were alive."

"Tabitha?"

"Mother Crum she were better knowed as." Tod gave a
backward glance. "If he be the owner it's him she left this to. A
nephew or somesuch. Come to think, the last time I seen that
key he were a-putting it in his pocket; and step-and-a-halfing it
to his car." He meant limping, but only as a joke, the man had
been laughing at the size and weight of the key. Bassett understood. His own back-door key was a monster.

They left the cottage, shut the door. Bassett stooped to inspect the keyhole: blocked by cobweb and desiccated wasp.
"You last touched this door when, Tod?"

"Year afore last." Tod repeated how and why he and Davey
had checked against break-ins.

"The door was locked, and you haven't approached the door
since, until today." Bassett pointed to the honesty. "This is
what attracted your attention."

"Ar," said Tod, meaning yes.

Bassett drew him down the garden towards the rhubarb
patch, pausing halfway to stand and look all round. His gaze
finally rested on the bundle of rhubarb sticks tied with string. "I

don't think I've ever tasted rhubarb wine," he said, after Tod had explained why he wanted the rhubarb. Didn't fancy it to tell the truth, he was a whisky, strong ale and grape-wine man himself.

"Good drop!" Tod said with a burst of enthusiasm. "Drop o' mine, you don't need no overcoat!"

Bassett grinned. "As good as that, eh? Righto, what do you want to do, finish your gathering while I nip home and phone? Won't take five minutes—"

But Tod could no more use that rhubarb now than he'd buy a dog from a gipsy. "I'm a-coming with you."

He'd a dread of coppers an' all, he confided as they drove up the lane, for they had travelled down in Bassett's Citroën. Been with him all his life, even when he were a lad and village bobbies were reputed to be Friends as well as Authority. No escaping the way you were made—and he was made to go all shifty-eyed and duthery if a bobby as much as blinked in his direction.

"You and half the general public," Bassett began reassuring him. But Tod was still speaking.

" 'Cepting you," he rumbled. "You're all right, but them with the pointed hats . . ." Anyroad, seeing as the mockers had been put on his wine-making . . . And seeing as Bassett was likely to be generous with his brandy . . . "Mebbe I could stay at your place, Harry, till they've been and gone."

"And mebbe you'd like a drink?" Bassett said, eyeing him sidelong. He knew Tod well. Crafty old devil.

"They're bound to want a statement," Bassett cajoled as he served the promised brandy. "I'll see the police first. I know most of your story, fill me in the gaps. The more I can pass on, the less they'll have to ask you."

So gaps were filled, Tod's glass refilled; and pup fell asleep on the old man's lap.

"The key," Bassett said. "People round here leave their doors unlocked." He was thinking of possible carelessness with keys. Had Tabitha been careless with hers?

Used to leave doors unlocked, Tod said. Not nowadays. And never Tabitha. She'd always had to be heedful of her mixtures and things.

Mixtures and things? "She was a cure-all?" Bassett said.

"A wise-woman, ar," Tod replied, using the country term.

Never left her door unlocked, never lost sight of her key, he explained; couldn't risk tomfoolery, the village wasn't without its practical jokers. And no, he never did any caretaking for Tabitha. And no, she never left the key in a plant pot or under a stone; for the very same reason that she never left her door unlocked. There was always some daft one who'd know where to look.

No, not even a spare.

"A spare left lying around forgotten—you don't think that's possible, then?" Bassett persisted gently.

"These keys never had spares, Harry. Made too big to get themselves lost. Carry one in a pocket and you knowed it were there. And when it weren't. Your door's an old 'un, dates back a bit—"

"True," Bassett agreed. "I've only the one key . . . There's only bare furniture in the cottage by the look of it, no knick-knacks or bits and pieces . . ."

Tod nodded lugubriously. "Arranged all that herself, did Tabitha. Knowed when her time was a-coming and fixed it up herself. I'd've liked to be planted in the woods, Tod, she says to me; like the birds and animals; but they won't let me. So she made her arrangements. Sold everything but what's left in there, put money aside for funeral costs 'cause she reckoned they'd make her have one, and booked herself into Rosemead Old Folks' Home with the rest. Weren't many weeks afore she got took. It'll last as long as me, Tod, she says; her bit of cash. Ar, and it did. Worked it out to the day, I reckon. Grand 'ooman," the old gamekeeper rumbled mournfully.

And then the question Bassett had been dying to ask. "Occurs to me the police will want to know why you went to

Tabitha's for rhubarb, you a countryman with a garden of your own . . . ?"

" 'Ten't no mystery, Harry. First drop of rhubarb wine I had off Tabitha, ooh! never tasted owt like it! Grand, it were. Champion." The dropped jaw, oval eyes, and lips pushed out to form a trunk expressed recollected joy bordering on ecstasy. "What you put in this, missus? I said . . ." Tod told his tale. In the process the colour was restored to his cheeks; and Bassett felt able to leave him.

He dialled the number of Glevebourne Police Station, asked to speak to Inspector Robert Greenaway.

The conversation was brief. Bob Greenaway returned the receiver to its rest, and turned to his sergeant, the amiable, outgoing Andy Miller. "Bassett," he complained. "Found a corpse, says the circumstances are suspicious. He's doing this on purpose, Andy. No serious crimes here, Snoopy moves in, and bump!—we're on overtime. I think he's touting for business on the quiet!"

FOUR

Alone in Crum Cottage, Bassett concentrated on the body. A part of him had no wish to get involved, it was a quiet life for him now. If anyone had asked, he was here solely for Tod's benefit, to smooth the path for the old gamekeeper. But murder had been his trade for a very long time—and there was something about this body that whispered murder now.

Whispered. Didn't shout from the rooftops like some bodies he'd seen. Didn't bare its wounds and scream for revenge. Whispered. Softly. Timidly almost.

And Bassett strained to hear.

True, it could have been as Tod had implied: the new owner let himself in, placed the key on the kitchen table, went through to the sitting-room, sat down feeling ill, and died where he sat.

There were no obvious signs of attack, but Bassett had noted previously the awkward positioning of one leg . . . the marks on the forehead underneath a plume of hair that had fallen over the brow . . . the staining—dried blood?—around the nostrils . . . the oddness about the chest. If Tod had seen any of this he might have attributed it to deterioration. Although it was more likely, as Bassett had guessed before, that Tod received little above an overall impression.

He was tempted to raise that one trouser leg, to lift that hair for a better look. Training and experience stayed his hand.

Moreover, how had the man got here? No car in the garage—he'd checked through a gap in the warped doors. Home from abroad? Car hire would have been Bassett's own choice. However, to each his own opinions and needs, so . . . Train, say, to Glevebourne, taxi from there. Or maybe he had been given a lift. To where—the door? Winter dress indicated winter weather and as many wet days as dry. Wet in the country was synonymous with muddy. Those shoes and trouser bottoms were reasonably clean, no discernible mud spots. At a guess the man hadn't walked far. And anyhow, that leg . . .

He looked at the portable gas fire in the fireplace: he had a similar fire himself, an efficient instant source of heat on frosty mornings. He visualized the man arriving, cold, sufficiently cold for him not to shed overcoat and gloves, and switching on the fire . . . Had the fire remained on until the gas ran out? Carefully, arms round the fire so as not to obliterate or add fingerprints, he lifted the thing bodily and shook it: there was gas in the cylinder. He lowered the fire to the ground, looked at the dead man. "What happened, old lad? So cold and weak you hadn't the energy to turn the gas on? It's a self-igniter so absence of matches would be no reason . . ."

Or did you switch it on—*and off again?*

Somehow this Bassett did not believe.

He looked behind the fire: no ash to speak of in the grate. He turned his own gas fire off once he'd a good log fire burning: no fire had been lit here. A small amount of paper had been burnt, wouldn't have warmed a flea. Besides, you don't light a fire immediately behind a gas cylinder, you shift the gas fire first.

And light. What about light? No electricity on. No candle or paraffin lamp in evidence. Perhaps it was daylight when the man arrived. But winter's days are short. Bassett gazed speculatively at the windows, the curtains . . . turned and moved to go upstairs.

For heaven's sake! He stopped, groaned aloud. What did he think he was doing! He shrugged, it was no use, Tod was right, you couldn't help the way you were made. He was made to snoop. He carried on upstairs.

Little to see. A wide dusty landing. Two bedrooms sparsely furnished. No trimmings. No towel or soap, or hint of anyone having slept here in years. Inserting his ballpoint in the open-work of a decorative handle, Bassett opened one wardrobe door and shut it again. The catch of a second wardrobe was loose. Both wardrobes were empty. If the man downstairs *was* the owner—no sign of luggage—he hadn't, on the face of it, come to stay.

Downstairs in the kitchen, using the ballpoint to open and shut fridge and cupboard doors, Bassett discovered a sealed bottle of whisky, a soda siphon and two tumblers in a cabinet; an empty whisky bottle and a paper handkerchief stained with lipstick in the pedal bin; and in a cupboard under the sink two Camping Gaz lamps and spare cylinders.

These finds had him returning to the sitting-room, where he now scrutinized the paper ash in the grate. An accumulation of biscuit wrappers, chocolate-box linings and such, innocuous rubbish to which some tidy-minded person had applied a match. Stale, dusty, there at least as long as the body, obviously. He noted the poker in the stand, resisted the temptation to give the paper ash a rake; and mused instead.

A gas fire for comfort . . . chocolates for my lady . . . two glasses . . . lamps for the dark hours. I wonder.

He was examining the quarry tiles on the entrance floor

when the shadow fell and a voice said, "I suppose your size fourteens have been all over the place!"

"Sure to be the truth!" Bassett looked up and smiled. "Didn't hear your car, Bob."

Bassett had lived in Oakleigh for some months before he located the nearest police station, six miles away in the small market town of Glevebourne. He went in one day: to satisfy himself that there was a local force, was his explanation, it had been so long since he'd seen a familiar blue uniform: to cure withdrawal symptoms, had been Mary's fond claim. At the station he had found Bob Greenaway, a sergeant from his past. Bob was an inspector here. They had worked together on the Wilson murder last autumn*—Bassett unofficially, of course— and had kept in touch ever since.

"Parked off the road and walked up," lean, dark-haired Inspector Greenaway said, as Bassett joined him and young Sergeant Miller outside. The ever-cheerful Andy Miller saluted a greeting. "That looked interesting, guvnor—"

"The floor? Faint drag marks, Andy. Could've been made by a single shoe—and the dead man has a game leg."

Bob Greenaway tut-tutted. "Just can't keep away, can you? Couldn't wait to retire and grow your own pork chops—but one whiff of murder and you're first on the scene!"

Bassett contrived to look innocent. "Who said anything about murder? The word I used was suspicious."

"Well, we'll soon know. Still keep pigs?" Greenaway said conversationally. "What are they called—Miss Piggy and Carter Brown?"

"Barrington-Smythe," Bassett corrected him, referring to the boar he'd named after a lawyer of his acquaintance. "Had to let them go, they got to be a handful. Remind me to tell you sometime about the day they got out. I spent a whole morning chasing them up and down the lane."

"Freezer?" Andy said hopefully.

* *Screaming Bones*

"Can't eat old friends!" Bassett reproached. "Last I saw of Barrington-Smythe he was throwing his weight around at Tyler's Farm. And Miss Piggy's living a life of luxury at John Stock's. She's in delicate condition," he added sedately.

"You're going to be an uncle!" announced Andy.

Bob Greenaway cocked a look, grinned, straightened his face. "Can't delay it any longer. I suppose we'd better."

Bassett led the way, stepping round the drag marks.

FIVE

Bassett pointed out the key on the kitchen table. "The owner of this cottage lives abroad, I understand. The body might be him come home. Or he could have left the key in somebody's safe-keeping. Either way it shouldn't be very difficult to identify the man."

They went through to the sitting-room. "No sign of a fight," Bob Greenaway said after surveying the room and the corpse. "Why suspicious, Harry?"

"For starters, I think there are injuries."

Bob Greenaway nodded. "The leg, for instance." He threw a look at the windows. "Curtains like that when you got here? One pair open, one pair shut . . . Why do they bother me?" he said quizzically.

"Because they present a tantalizing puzzle. You want to know if it was day or night when the man arrived. Had he started to open the curtains—or close them."

"Or were they like that when he came in," Greenaway said. "The chap who found him . . . ?"

"Tod Arkwright. He's at my place."

"Tod Arkwright?" Andy slid a sideways grin to Bassett. "I think I know him. Spins yarns to tourists in the village pub, they buy him ale. Bought him a pint myself one night, found out later he hates coppers."

"So he says," Bassett said, returning the grin. "I'm beginning not to believe it. He's a friend of mine, too."

"What's his story?"

"Rhubarb," Bassett said. "He's been coming here for years for rhubarb to make wine, he and the old lady whose cottage this was were buddy-pals. Why here? Because this particular rhubarb is special. The old lady was a cure-all, much respected in her day. She made all her own medicaments, and if you believe Tod wasn't averse to chanting a spell over them. Her rhubarb wine? He'd never tasted a wine like it! Thought she had some secret ingredient, but she never would tell. Came the day she went off her feet and couldn't do her brewing herself she gave Tod a bundle of rhubarb, yeast and a bag of sugar, asked him to brew it for her. The secret ingredient? There wasn't one. The fine flavour was in the rhubarb itself." Bassett didn't mock, and neither did they.

"The soil," Bob Greenaway said. Bassett agreed. Grapes varied. Grape wines varied from region to region; why not rhubarb? "Anyhow, old Tod's used this rhubarb ever since . . . Tabitha Crum, if you want to make a note.

"After the old lady died, five or six years ago, he received permission from the new owner to carry on as he'd always done. He usually came by the back lane, got his rhubarb and left the same way. Only on three occasions in five years has he approached the back door. The first was shortly after he met the new owner—he tapped on the door in case anyone was home. The second was a couple of years ago when antique thieves were in the area. He tried the door then—it was locked. The third time was today, after he spotted the honesty—the flowers by the back step—"

"Honesty? From a teller of tall tales?" An eyebrow went up.

Bassett shook his head and smiled. "Makes sense to me, Bob. Will to you too when you go and see."

The other motioned. "Show me. Any excuse for a breath of freshers . . . These?"—when they were outside.

"Yeah. Tod's daughter has taken up flower-arranging. Asked

her dad to watch out for some, seems our old cottage garden flowers are becoming rare. She wants the seed heads in the autumn. They make excellent decorative material, apparently, when they've dried out."

"He's right, guv," Andy told the inspector. "We've got some in our front room. My ma calls it angels' wings. I've never seen it growing before. Look! Little green seed heads already!"

"OK, OK," Bob Greenaway grouched. "We don't want a botany lesson. Like a pair of old women."

"Tod had never seen any *here* before," Bassett said. "But he spotted this clump, came for a look-see, sniffed—tried the door, found it unlocked."

"Locked two years ago—unlocked today." Bob Greenaway pursed his lips. "That's what you said, Harry. You're suggesting the body could have been in there for up to two years—?"

"His clothes indicate winter, Bob. Last winter? I don't believe so. I think the winter before. Body's had time to dry out a little."

"Which amounts to the same thing," said Andy. "But a door unlocked for that length of time, no call for anyone to open it? Is that possible?"

"Round here, yes. Quite possible."

"This Tod—" There was a peculiar gleam in Bob Greenaway's eyes. "He didn't recognize the man?"

Bassett shook his head. "No, but it is five years since he saw the owner, and he only met him the once. And at the risk of stating the obvious—"

Bob Greenaway interrupted. "Cast your minds back." He shot a look from Bassett to Andy and back again. "Got it? Christmas before last?"

It took Andy a second; then, "Oh hell!"

From Bassett a series of puppet-like nods as a slow understanding began to dawn. Vague recollections. He and Mary had gone to France for a month, to spend the Christmas period with her brother. There had been snippets on the news after they

returned. Updates. Negatives. He hadn't paid too much attention, other things on his mind. Mary. "A judge went missing
from Hereford while Mary and I were away. His car was found
at Glevebourne Railway Station . . ." He jabbed at the air with
a finger. "You think . . . ?"

"Never did find him," Bob Greenaway growled. "Vanished
off the face of the earth."

Car noise and voices diverted their attention. " 'Bout time."
Bob Greenaway greeted the photographer. "Jim, get cracking.
The usual of the body as fast as you can so that I can get to his
pockets."

White-haired, sports-jacketed Dr. Jim McPherson, police
surgeon, made eyes at Bassett and Andy Miller, then grinned.
"Panic stations? Stale one, they tell me. Been here a long
time—"

Bob Greenaway cut in. "Jim, I want to know how long. Soon
as you can. Want to know if we're talking about anything like
eighteen months." He spoke with urgency.

"Definitely panic stations," Doc mumbled, trudging after the
photographer. "Who is he—do we know?"

"We think he could be Judge Jeffries," Andy Miller replied,
following him in.

The contents of the dead man's wallet identified him as Hugh
Ainsley Jeffries, aged forty-three, with an address at Bath. Doc
McPherson confirmed that he could have been dead for as long
as eighteen months.

When, shortly afterwards, Doc informed them that the
corpse appeared to have in layman's terms a busted kneecap,
some cracked ribs, a depression on the forehead, possibly a
fracture; and agreed that, yes, the injuries could be consistent
with a beating, Bob Greenaway first exploded the name of
those he thought responsible: "The Smiths!"—and then voiced
the opinion that the body had probably been dumped.

Bassett was unaware of this. He was curious, most certainly;
but they didn't need his interference. While the team was

around, Bob might even resent his erstwhile gaffer's presence. He snooped in the back garden for a time, not looking for anything in particular, and finding nothing more exciting than an abandoned cache of partly-eaten hazel nuts and rose hips low down in the drystone wall. He wondered idly what small creature had been hibernating there, mouse, dormouse, and what had disturbed it. For the wall had started crumbling here, some additional light force having completely dislodged a lump of rock, exposing the hidey-hole to the elements and predators. But he thought better of showing his find to the poker-face on duty in the garden. Not everyone appreciated his interest in wildlife.

Instead, when it became plain that nobody was coming to fetch him in he touched his hat, said a courteous good day to the constable, and took himself off.

It was left to Doc McPherson, long after Andy Miller had been for Tod Arkwright's statement and given Tod a ride home, to tell Bassett what was going on.

Bassett was standing by his garden gate looking up and down a deserted lane, pup sticky-beaking through the bars below, when the telephone rang.

"Thought I'd give you a tinkle," Doc said, "in case you wondered why I hadn't dropped by. Andy Miller said he was coming to interview the chap who found the body. I didn't want to intrude."

"Would have been no intrusion, Jim. Pleased you've phoned, though. *Is* it Judge Jeffries?"

"Good lord! Didn't Andy tell you?"

"Told me nothing," Bassett said, sounding sorry for himself. "Asked Tod if the name Jeffries meant anything to him, a few questions about the key; just kept grinning at me."

Doc chuckled. "Oh dear. I fancy they thought you'd put your own two and two together. Well, it seems to be Jeffries. Credit and club cards in his wallet. Nothing for you this time, I fear. Case all cut and dried as far as I can make out."

"Jim—Mary and I were in France when the Judge disappeared. I'm in ignorance, knew none of the background to the case . . ."

Doc read him well.

Apparently Judge Jeffries, a circuit judge, had finished his stint at Hereford Crown Court eighteen months previously, seventeen to be precise, packed his bags, wished staff at Judges' Residence a happy Christmas, and to all intents and purposes set off for his home in Bath. He wasn't married, had no one actually waiting for him, so no one noticed when he failed to turn up.

Three days later, on Tuesday, December 20th, Glevebourne Police received a call from the local railway station. A BMW in their car park, been there for three days. The car was identified as belonging to Hugh Jeffries. A suitcase and the box in which the Judge kept his wig and robes were in the boot. The car was undamaged.

Hugh Jeffries's sister had been about to go to the police, she said when notified. She was his only close relative, close in the sense that they were related, for they saw each other infrequently and had little in common. Nevertheless, Hugh was well-mannered, Wanda Jeffries averred, and a keeper of promises. He had promised his assistance with a party of deprived children being treated to a Christmas outing. When he failed to put in an appearance or to contact her with an explanation or apology, and neither his live-out housekeeper nor his known associates were able to throw light on his whereabouts, she had begun to worry. The more so after his colleagues acquainted her with the so-called threats made by the Smiths.

"Who are—?"

"Settled gipsies," said Doc.

Aaron and Isaac Smith had been accused of manslaughter and theft after an elderly widow, Rosie Hayward, living on the outskirts of Hereford, had been found dead in her home. Rosie had died of a cerebral haemorrhage, but a ransacked house, various items missing, suggested that she had died during the execution of a crime. A neighbour reported seeing the two Smith brothers at the house a day or so earlier. They were later caught with Rosie's valuable porcelain collection in their possession.

The brothers swore their innocence, swore that Rosie had given them the porcelain on the day the neighbour saw them, and that they were never there on the night she died. But in the absence of an alibi they were not believed; the manslaughter charge was dropped, but they were charged with burglary, convicted, and sent down for seven years.

"Which resulted in an uproar in court," Doc said. "The Smiths and supporters accused the Judge of bias when he directed the jury. They threatened him—"

"Ergo, when he disappeared," Bassett observed, "the consensus was that the threats had been carried out. The gipsy equivalent of a concrete overcoat. Right? D'you know who handled it, Jim?"

"County police. Glevebourne's only concern was the BMW. I was asking Andy about the case this afternoon. The Smith family were suspected of having a hand in the Judge's disappearance, but there was insufficient evidence to justify any arrest."

"Mm. As I recall," Bassett said, "our local railway station is small. Leisurely flow of passengers. Generous parking. Meaning no fist fights over parking space. Car parked long term should have stood out. How come it took three days to spot the BMW?"

It didn't, it took three days to *report* it. Doc reminded Bassett that no one was looking for the car, the Judge hadn't been reported missing at the time. The BMW had aroused no great curiosity from railway staff for two days. It wasn't unusual for a passenger to leave a car overnight, little to fear from vandals here.

But snow had started falling in the early hours of the third day. And when you see a car covered with undisturbed snow, that is when you stop and think. Hasn't that been there for a couple of days? Think we ought to check up?

"That was when the ball started rolling," Doc said. "Although it caused only a small stir, Christmas coming up. A name on a missing persons list here. Till now. Now it's Robert's case, all cut and dried, as I say; killers ready to be dished up on a plate."

"Killers? We are talking about murder, then?"

With his injuries, unlikely to be anything else, Doc said. Busted ribs, kneecap, forehead. Consistent with a beating. Therefore the same applied now as eighteen months ago. As long as the dead man was Hugh Jeffries, the Smith family were prime suspects.

"Any doubt about his identity?" Bassett inquired.

"Not really. Compare the facial bone structure with the excuse they've got for a photograph, and I think it's Hugh Jeffries. And it all ties in so far."

Cause of death couldn't be determined until Doc had the body on the slab. Could be internal bleeding. But there was a strong possibility that the dead man received more than one blow to the forehead by more than one instrument, and that one of the blows had been the death blow.

Which added weight to the theory that the man had been given a good hiding. Put in boot and dumped.

One thing was certain, Doc said; with that kneecap he didn't walk anywhere.

And his car had been found at the railway station.

They talked a few minutes longer, ended the call.

Thirty seconds ticked away. Bassett picked up the receiver and dialled Doc's number. "Why *dumped,* Jim?"

"The police believe some of the Smith family may have lined up the cottage beforehand, while prospecting for scrap and antiques. You know, rubbish shoved into barns and outhouses. Went to Crum Cottage two or three times, never anybody about, found an old key which fitted the lock, and well, whether they stole anything from the premises or not, they had the perfect place to drop poor Jeffries when he died on them."

"I see. Thank you, Jim. Sorry to have brought you back to the phone."

But Doc didn't go immediately. "You don't like it," he said succinctly. He could tell by the tone of Bassett's voice. "Like when you were a kid? When the answers were at the back of the book? That it?"

Bassett grunted. "Back of the book was all right. I did used to beef when they were on the same page."

"Gipsies threaten Judge, Judge dies, gipsies must have done it. Too simple?"

Bassett sighed. " 'Tis only me, Jim. When I viewed the body I was without benefit—or as may turn out to be the case, disadvantage—of preconception. I saw things *only as they were.*"

Later, evening chores done, Bassett sank into his big wraparound leather armchair, the one Mary had affectionately called his security blanket, the one beautifully moulded to his shape, and filled a pipe. A thinking pipe. A sleepy pup climbed onto his lap, roused herself to gaze adoringly into his eyes and bestow several moist licks, then curled up, nose tucked under his armpit, safe and warm. Bassett stroked her soft coat, and pondered.

Dusk. The chirring of starling fledglings calling for their supper from the roof of his porch coincided with the arrival of a brown owl on a branch of his old cherry tree. The night shift were preparing to take over when Bassett's deliberations came to an end.

"Consider the implications, babydog. A fire for make-do comfort . . . drinks for two . . . an element of secrecy. *But* only one pair of curtains drawn—and a man fully-clothed even to his gloves. I'd think of an angry husband before I'd think of vengeful gipsies."

Pup's response was a loud snore. "I agree," Bassett said softly. "Let's sleep on it."

He had to get up in the middle of the night: a toilet trip for pup. It was while he was standing bleary-eyed on the porch step waiting for her that it came to him: gipsies *had* been in the area at around the time of Hugh Jeffries's disappearance.

SIX

Sally was quietly full of it next morning. No gossip, his cleaning lady, as she was forever reminding people; yet Bassett obtained all the village news from her.

"They've found that missing Judge, then!" she exclaimed as she tied on her apron, one Bassett hadn't seen before, heavily patterned with roses. "Bit gaudy for me, really," she remarked. "But Julie made it. Anyway it's bright and cheerful!" As was she. Whatever yesterday's worry, Sally wasn't showing it now. "Fancy him being in Tabitha Crum's all this time!"

Good grief! Bassett thought. A village that sprawled, houses and farms often remote, yet bad news seemed to travel more rapidly than along a street of doorstep busybodies.

"Not that the name meant much to me," Sally went on, after Bassett had admired the apron, which was in fact quite pretty. "I couldn't even remember Hanging Judge Jeffries till they reminded me. Poor old Tod, though. It shook him up, didn't it?"

Bassett met her eyes briefly: they were twinkling, telling all. He could imagine. Once Andy's questions had sunk in, Tod would have had a high old time capitalizing on his experience, a pick-me-up at every garden gate.

"Don't rightly know who it is, he said. Could be somebody named Jeffries. Jeffries? Jeffries?"—voice rising to a squeak. "Well, everybody started remembering then."

" 'Cept me, Sally. Mary and I were out of the country when the Judge vanished. And you omitted to fill us in when we got back."

She matched his mock-woeful expression with her own.

"Didn't know you well then, did I?" He had been someone who flitted in now and then and pulled his wife's leg and hers, or made them laugh doing his country bumpkin act, no offence intended. "Don't suppose it entered my head, to tell the truth. Christmas, wasn't it? Christmas before last. A lot happens at Christmas when you've a brood the size of mine. I probably told you all about the parties and the squabbles."

"Yes, I think you probably did."

"Not as there was much to remember, Mr. B. They found his car at the railway station—that was on Police 5 one tea-time. And I think there was a bit in the *Gazette*. But it wasn't *our* news, if you understand me, he didn't come from round here, wasn't one of *us* . . . Had a stroke or something, didn't he?" she said, voice rising again as she started bustling.

"Don't know what he died of yet, Sally."

"They're saying the gipsies did it, the Smiths. Put the hex on him! Well, Tod says that—some of the others are saying the gipsies killed him because he sent two of the lads to gaol! Not as I believe that myself, not if they're the Smiths as come round here!"

Bassett waited until she drew her head out of the broom cupboard. "Selling what, Sally?"

"Not selling, Mr. B—buying. Furniture, antiques, bric-à-brac, scrap—"

"Know them well, do you?"

"Not as to say well, Mr. B, but they've been in these parts a good number of years and never given trouble, I do know. Gave up travelling ages ago. Keep a farm or something on the road to Ross, as well as the other businesses. Never do more than knock on your door or call to you from the gate, the Smiths! You never catch them ferreting on the sly like you do some of them didecoys . . . ! They came here once!" Activity ceased for Bassett to be fed a look. "Had a lorry piled high with junk, old mangles and that. I say junk—" Sally ticked herself off. "Museum pieces they are now, mangles. Big ugly Victorian bath they had, too. Fetch a fortune, they do. When I think of the

stuff my lot have thrown out or burnt on bonfires!" she said
with a rueful sigh. Then her voice went up again. "The owd'un
was with them, usually it's just two of the lads. He was more
interested in your pigs, remember? Chatting for ages by the
pigsty, you were."

Bassett remembered. "Called me boss." And plucked black-
berries from an adjacent bush while they chin-wagged. He'd
been wrong last night, they hadn't been in the area around
Christmas time, must have been late summer.

"I must admit I never connected the Smiths as come round
here with the court case," Sally continued, sorting dusters.
"Robbed some old lady, didn't they? Different Smiths altogether, I thought. Now, though, well—different again, isn't it?
Is it right the door was left open?"

"Not open. Unlocked."

"Julie could be right then, she said it could have been anybody. If anything was done by anybody," she said, quizzing
him. And getting nowhere.

"I've known the time you could leave your door wide open,"
she went on, "and nobody'd walk in uninvited. Now they not
only walk in, they walk out again with anything they can carry.
Some cheeky devils'll even dig your fireplace out and hump it
off. The things my sister Doris's told me! She lives in a city, but
as she says, everywhere's getting to be the same."

God forbid! "I don't think anything was stolen from Crum
Cottage," Bassett ventured.

"Added more like," Sally said. "Gas fire in her best room,
wasn't there? That was never Ma Crum's. Ooh no! Wouldn't
have had gas anywhere near her plants and medicines . . .
Anyway, this won't do. You are an old gossip, you know." She
trotted off.

Since Sally wouldn't hear of him helping with the polishing,
and anyhow pup would want to join in, result chaos, Bassett
occupied himself outdoors. He watched an occasional police
car drive past, waited for one to stop; none did. No routine
questions for him.

A telephone call would have sufficed. But why should Bob Greenaway ring him up if he already had the case sewn up? If the dead man *was* Judge Jeffries?

When at last the telephone did ring Doc McPherson was on the other end of the line. The body had been formally identified by Wanda Jeffries. A scar ruled out any doubt. Members of the Smith clan were being brought in for questioning.

"I can push ahead with the autopsy now," Doc said. "Anything you personally want me to look for?"

"I'd be interested to know if he had an existing game leg, Jim."

"Noted."

"And Jim—?" The pause was brief but marked. "Keep an open mind."

"Will do," was the firm reply.

"I wonder if he was a relative?" Sally said, when they had their elevenses. "Judge Jeffries? A relation of Tabitha's. I mean, somebody must have given somebody the key. Be different if they'd broken into the place. I mean, nobody'd heard of this nephew Tabitha left the cottage to. What if another relation thought it should have been his?—and he heard about the trouble with the Smiths in court, and took the opportunity?"

To bump the legatee off? Hoping the Smiths would carry the can?

"Anything is possible," Bassett said. Implied that the so-called nephew and Hugh Jeffries were one and the same, though . . .

Sally herself changed the subject by plucking up the courage to tell Bassett her problem. No problem at all, really. It was her granddaughter. "Julie wants to join the police, Mr. B, and she wondered if you would give her a reference. I feel awkward asking. You don't know her. I mean, I . . . well . . . you know . . ."

"You mean how could I be expected to supply a reference to

someone I've never met? I know you, Sally, and if you vouch for
the girl . . . Good girl, is she?"

"Got brains as well. More than her gran ever had!"

"Tell me about her." They discussed Julie, her life, school-
ing, ambitions, where she worked. "Davis's Garage. On the
other side of Glevebourne—know where I mean? Big place,
Mr. B. Showroom, shop. They do MOTs, and car hire, and all
that. But there're no career prospects for Julie, and girls aren't
content nowadays just to bide time until they get married . . ."

Car. Car hire. Bassett felt faint stirrings at the back of his
mind: a shuffling among the mountains of information he had
filed away over the years, often subliminally, under the heading
"experience." He began thinking of the Judge's injuries in
relation to a car accident rather than a beating . . . For the
moment these had to be just passing thoughts. He let them go.

"Spends most of her time on the pumps, did you say?"

"Mm," Sally said wretchedly. "No recommendation, is it,
Mr. B?"

"It has much to recommend it," Bassett said kindly. "She's
learning to deal with people, for one thing. That is an art in
itself. When she has her application forms tell her to come and
see me."

Sally was delighted. Bassett met the twinkle in her eyes with a
similar in his. "What about Mother Crum? Did you know her
well?" His smile was warm with anticipation.

But Sally shook her head. "I think I've told you before, I
come from a few miles away, moved here when I married, never
did join her circle of friends."

So much for the "old gossip." When he made a genuine
attempt he was a dead loss.

"I'll tell you one thing, though," Sally said later. "Don't
know where I've got the idea from, but I'm sure I heard the
gipsies wouldn't go anywhere near Crum's."

Bassett had thought to pay another visit to Crum Cottage, but he never did manage it that day. Frank Wood, retired blacksmith and octogenarian father of Archie, landlord of the Golden Pheasant, Oakleigh's village pub, was the first of a stream of droppers-by.

"Bad business, Bassett—" jerking his head in the general direction of Crum Cottage, sighing, and putting on a face. "I knew Tabitha well, you know." As if it was Tabitha whose body had been found.

"What was she, Frank—ministering angel? Unofficial midwife and nurse?" Bassett inquired politely.

"More in the doctoring line," Frank informed. "Made all her own medicaments pre-National Health. And after, for some of us." He sucked his teeth. Sucked his teeth at every pause. Then made the next thing he said sound like an announcement. "Cure for everything!" Pause. "If 'er didn't cure you, you didn't have it to begin with!" Pause. "Grew all her own ingredients! Most of 'em, anyroad." Pause. "T'others she got from Nature's garden, the woods and the meadows!"

"Something I miss, seeing Tabitha pottering round the lanes." They had been joined by Dick Webster, redundant farm-worker turned freelance odd-job man. "Always ready for a laugh, Tabitha."

Mr. Glass, out with his collie, stopped for a chat. Audrey Stokes just happened to be passing, miles off course. A couple Bassett knew by sight fibbed that as they'd missed the wild daffodils, the bluebells were a must . . . "Had some excitement, haven't you? Police cars . . ." their little old hearts dying for a share in it. Any minute the lame and the halt would arrive carried on their beds, Bassett thought a trifle facetiously as the ground both sides of the gate began to look crowded.

Mrs. Hardy from Foxgloves appeared, walking her scottie dog *up* the lane, a rare occurrence. "I used to take Tabs a dinner in, you know . . ."

"Never heard her mention a judge," said someone else.

Therein lay the reason for Bassett's popularity on this particular afternoon: the weather had brought them out, they all said; but all of them were fishing. No harm intended, no malicious intent. A form of morbid curiosity, but also a means of obtaining verification; police asked questions without explaining why, and you couldn't rely on everything Tod Arkwright said.

Bassett didn't mind. He submitted happily to being talked *around,* not to; listened, nodded intelligently now and then; and gleaned information. Information about Mother Crum, granted, but his visitors hadn't known Hugh Jeffries or the nephew, so they could hardly talk about *them* . . . The title Mother appeared to have been what it normally was, an affectionate form of address awarded to women of certain age and standing; Tabitha was unmarried, and there was no intimation of a child born out of wedlock (who might have been Jeffries); no known reason why the Judge should be in the cottage; no hint of a connection with gipsies, except insofar as the old lady used to be friendly with gipsies in the days when they sold pegs and scrounged hazel rods from which pegs were made . . . No sighting of a BMW. Or activity suspicious or otherwise in the vicinity of Crum Cottage eighteen months ago. Or at any time, come to that.

On the face of it nothing whatsoever to aid a murder inquiry, but useful information nevertheless.

Jessie, village milk lady and wife of Jan, a Polish wartime RAF pilot, both close friends of Bassett's, arrived after the impromptu tea-party had broken up.

"Brought your bill, but it's only an excuse to be nosey," she said, hitching up baggy trousers as they went into the kitchen. "Busy afternoon, I hear." She had met some stragglers in the lane.

"Inundated," Bassett exaggerated, grinning. "Everybody anxious to tell me about Tabitha Crum."

Jessie frowned. "Why Tabitha?"

"None of them knew the Judge."

"Ah!" Aping him.

"Used me as a focal point. Talked around me as if I was the village pump."

Jessie giggled. "Learnt all you need?"

Bassett moved his head noncommittally.

"Shame," Jessie said soberly. "In there all that time and nobody knowing. Anybody see him? Before, I mean?"

"Apparently not. Seems to have got there in absolute secrecy."

"Wouldn't be difficult, would it, on this stretch? There has been a yellow Ford parked on that patch of grass just below Crum's some early mornings, but I think you'll find it was a pal of Tommy Martin's, when they were out rabbiting." Jessie frowned again. "I can't think of anything that might help."

"Mother Crum," Bassett said. "I have a picture of a sweet old lady, well-versed in country wisdom, who never married—her young man was killed in the First World War and who had no known surviving relatives other than the mysterious nephew."

Jessie had little to add, she said; although there was much more to Tabitha than that. She was clever, had loads of books, *and* read them. Her folk had lived hereabouts on and off for generations, one day rich, another day poor. Latterly they had been teachers, missionaries, that kind of thing. "No longer much money but plenty of grace," Jessie said. "That clearing in the woods, as you cut across to the blackcurrant plantation— used to be a house there belonging to Tabitha's people. Nothing but wild flowers now. I think she was what they call the last of the line.

"And I *think*—between you and me—that the nephew isn't a nephew. I think he's related to the man she was going to marry. I bet he looks like her young man. She had some photographs of him. Brings a lump to your throat, doesn't it? Lovely lady, she was."

Bassett poured Jessie a glass of cider while she was speaking. Now she drank it, said, "Delicious! Thank you," and rinsed the glass under the tap. "He wasn't—isn't—a judge, I know that for certain. And if there had been a judge in the family I'm positive she'd have said."

She glanced at the clock on the wall. "Late for my hair appointment again! Annie'll murder me . . . Shouldn't say that, should I? Not with two down, one to go . . . The rule of three," she enlarged when Bassett looked blank. "Derek Wilson last year, now the Judge . . ."

"Ah!" Bassett caught on. "Six months between, Jess."

She laughed. "Oh, it'll still count. That means nothing round here. We're so slow it would take that long to catch up with ourselves. As my dad used to say—get a punch on the nose, it takes some of us a fortnight to fall down!"

Bassett laughed with her. Then saw her out. "See you tonight!" she called over her shoulder as she sprinted to her Land-Rover.

Bassett reflected: Was it really possible for the Judge's body to have been sitting in Crum Cottage through the turmoil of the Wilson case?

Yes. Yes, he had to be honest: it was.

SEVEN

"See you tonight," Jessie had said. On Friday nights, except during the most popular summer months, when tourists abounded, Bassett and village friends were accustomed to gather in the Pheasant for a social evening. Jessie and husband Jan. The Reverend Willy Brewerton. Charlie Allsop, egg producer. Tod. Jack Carter . . . Charlie's old mother, Winnie, would have been the one to talk to if he'd needed to know more about Tabitha Crum; but Jack knew gipsies.

As the afternoon drew to a close and Bassett gave pup her supper, the hens their tea-time corn, and locked them up for the night, it was Jack who dominated his thoughts.

Jack. Jack the Poacher, who had returned to his roots after a forty-year absence and now owned and ran a bird sanctuary. Jack had grown up in Oakleigh, a ragamuffin who had lived as much by his wits as by the sweat of his young labours; until the Second World War, when he had rushed into uniform. He had made officer in the field, and later . . . But never mind the man's army and government career. Jack had once upon a time been champion among poachers; knew every inch of these hills, knew everyone who lived close to the earth. Knew, loved, and wrote about them in books and country articles.

Bassett was cleaning pup's demolition zone, that corner of the kitchen where she ate, when Jack came on the telephone.

"Harry, this Jeffries affair. Little bird tells me you were there. Are you working on it?"

"Why?"

"I want to pick your brains."

"Pick away."

"If you're going to the Pheasant, fancy a plod cross-country? I've had someone with me for the past couple of hours. Daniel Smith, head of the Smith gipsy clan . . ."

They arranged to rendezvous at the clearing Jessie had spoken about, but long before he reached the spot Bassett saw the unmistakable figure of the bearded giant he liked and respected coming to meet him.

They shook hands warmly. From Jack: "Did I detect a lack of surprise on the phone?" A counter from Bassett: "Didn't you write an article on gipsies recently?"

"Reminiscences, Harry. Written from memory and all the more colourful because of it, I hope. Although Dan's wife . . ." The beard spread round a grin. "You must meet her sometime." He tapped the pockets of his green belted jacket, apologizing to pup for forgetting the choc drops, and stooped down to her level. She found his beard fascinating: some strange playful animal that didn't flinch from her exploring nose.

"I thought Daniel Smith might be with you," Bassett said.

"No." The Poacher nuzzled pup one more time, then disentangled her from his beard and stood up. "I'll be doing what I can to help him, but if you could do anything about this latest . . . He says the police seem determined to pin Judge Jeffries's death on his people."

"You're familiar with what happened eighteen months ago, Jack?"

"I am now. Daniel's told me their side of things."

"Only now? I thought you might have known them in the old days. Might have followed the case."

"I knew Daniel and Fleur, yes. They were romantic characters then—gipsies who lived in caravans drawn by horses. Camp fires. Tales of adventure. Romance goes when they move into houses. To my shame, I neglected to look them up when I came back. Dan, however, got wind of me. And today, when the police started questioning his people all over again he hunted me out."

"Anyone held? Arrested?"

"No," Jack said. "They're treading old ground. I think they'll have their work cut out. According to Daniel, no stone was left unturned when the Judge disappeared . . . Nothing has changed."

They headed towards the gentle slope of the lower hill, Bassett waiting until they were clear of last year's bracken and tangled undergrowth before letting pup off her lead: adders were plentiful and lively, pup as inquisitive as her master.

"Can you tell me about the porcelain allegedly stolen by— was it Daniel's sons?"

"Grandsons," Jack said. "Aaron and Ike."

It had all started with a clock. "Rosie, the Hereford lady, had a chap knock on her door offering cash for the clock on her mantelshelf. Spotted it one night when her light was on, the very clock he'd been looking for! Wanted it so badly he was prepared to pay over the odds for it. You know the spiel. Offered Rosie a hundred pounds. Which frightened the old girl—"

"Frightened her?"

"Worried her," Jack amended. "Old-fashioned honesty. As far as she was concerned, the clock was only worth a few pounds; she couldn't take a hundred, she'd be cheating the man. As luck would have it, Aaron and Ike were in the district. Out of curiosity—she'd told the con merchant she'd think about it—she showed the clock to Aaron. He told her the truth —if authentic the clock could fetch a thousand pounds. He put her in touch with a dealer, she received a fair price, and tootled off to Australia to see her only son. Like winning the pools! She couldn't thank Aaron enough.

"Aaron and Ike thought no more about it, other than that they had gained a friend. Whenever they were in the area after that Rosie would fetch them in for a drink.

"Then about two years ago she approached Aaron at some trotting races. She was there with neighbours, a day out. I've something I want you and your brother to have, she told Aaron; a small thank-you. Presumably for the favour they had done her all those years previously. She had suffered a mild stroke, the next might see her off altogether; she knew they liked pottery and she had some to give them while she was of sound mind, then there would be no argument . . . She told Aaron she had inherited the porcelain from an aunt who had inherited it from a grandmother. Came to me in a laundry basket, she said, packed in newspaper, and there it's been ever since, gathering dust in my spare bedroom.

"What she gave them was an old Victorian laundry basket filled with newspaper-wrapped bundles, with throwaway junk items on top. Like a job lot at an auction. There, she said, just as it came to me.

"Now—this is what helped to put them behind bars—they didn't look at what they had for thirty-six hours; had in fact just started unwrapping the stuff when police walked in and caught them—guilt all over their faces.

"According to Daniel, it wasn't guilt but something else— shock among other things. Because if the rest was as valuable as the first two pieces, what Rosie had given them was worth a small fortune—"

"Hold it there a moment," Bassett said. "They were told the porcelain had been handed down through several generations —and they didn't *look* at it?"

"The very point the prosecution made much of," Jack said. "Apparently when Aaron and Ike were questioned they told it as it was, even to the 'just as it came to me.' Strictly speaking, Rosie probably meant what she'd said: wrapped in newspaper, packed in a basket, all there, every piece, intact. The police, it seems, took it literally. The porcelain was wrapped—but in newspapers less than six months old. They maintained that Aaron and Ike were re-wrapping the porcelain to give credence to a story they concocted after they learnt that Rosie died as a result of a burglary. A burglary committed by them—"

"Committed when?" Thirty-six hours . . . "The night after she had given them the porcelain?"

Affirmed. "Always supposing—I'm stating the prosecution view—the porcelain had been in the gift basket . . . All neighbours saw being carried out was a basket full of junk."

"Which may have been what Rosie wanted them to think," Bassett said, after a moment's thought. "All the same, why the delay in having a peep?"

"Busy, all manner of things going on. But when it comes down to it, blame the wrappings," said Jack. "If they had been yellow with age, Aaron and Ike would undoubtedly have sneaked a look. As it was, Rosie's house was in a state, half-empty when they collected the basket; china cabinet and shelves virtually stripped bare. They thought she'd parcelled up plates and ornaments she'd had displayed, nice, but mass-produced, and fantasized a little to make them sound better than they were. Because she wanted them to have something *worthwhile.* They had a smile over it—dear Rosie, the stroke had sent her slightly dotty, she might even have come to believe *all* her possessions were treasures; the clock had been, why not everything else."

"Makes sense," Bassett said.

"According to Daniel," Jack continued, "the lads only accepted the gift so as not to upset Rosie. They had it in mind eventually to take the pieces back to her a few at a time, pretending they'd come across them in a sale and thought she might like to have them."

"And wouldn't recognize them as being the same pieces she had given them, eh?"

"Something like that."

At the flat top of the first rise they halted, gazed down at the myriad greens all around them; an evening glow on a field of fluorescent yellow rape on one horizon, a mist hugging the mountains of Wales on another; watched a walker being swallowed up by a leaf-canopied path below them; and resumed walking themselves.

"The son in Australia—" Bassett began.

"As far as Daniel has been able to make out, he was informed of his mother's death by the family solicitor. Didn't show up at the court or the funeral. So we don't know if he was aware of the value of the porcelain or not. Rosie herself may not have known. Not all old stuff is valuable."

"And Daniel's grandsons presumably never saw any of the collection until Rosie gave it to them?"

"Apparently not," Jack said. "The prosecution turned their defence upside down. Made strong suggestions that they *did* know about the porcelain; that it was they who approached Rosie after her stroke, took advantage of her incapacity, and conned her out of her treasure."

"And then went back . . ." Bassett said dubiously.

"Because she *hadn't* given them the porcelain, was the prosecution's claim. She *had* given them cheap ornaments, did give them a basket of junk; she switched the contents."

"And they went back for the genuine article. I see. A case of who do you believe, the accused or the accusers."

They came to their own downward path, precarious in parts

but no deterrent to pup, who bounded down using her otter-like tail as a rudder. Bassett next, single file.

"Daniel's people are Romany," Jack said, loudly so as to be heard above the noise of crackling twigs underfoot.

"Meaning they're tribal," Bassett called over his shoulder.

"Yes." They were on a level now, room to walk side by side. "Tribal laws can be stricter than legal laws. Break the family code, the whole family sits in judgement. And vice versa. Aaron and Ike have the full support of the family. Meaning the family found them innocent even though a jury did not."

"And so the family protested—threatened the Judge."

"Cursed him," Jack said. "Told him he'd live to rue the day, that's all. Wasn't meant to do more than put the wind up him for a day or two."

"Many a true word spoken in jest," Bassett murmured.

" 'Fraid so. I'm going to have a go at proving Aaron and Ike's innocence," Jack said. "There's a question of a letter to the son from Rosie telling him what she planned to do with the porcelain. I'll tell you more when I've had a chat with one of her neighbours . . ."

"And if I could find out what really happened to the Judge. That what you want to ask?" Bassett said.

"Well, I can't see you sitting on your backside letting the police do all the work," Jack replied with a grin.

"Police tell Daniel how he died? No? Can't tell you specifics until after the autopsy, but it looks as if he was given a good hiding. And he could well have been in Crum Cottage for the entire eighteen months that he was missing."

"As I said—nothing has changed."

Bassett asked: "Did you know Tabitha Crum in the old days, Jack?"

"Gave me some jollop for a sick owl once."

"Mmm." They walked on in step. "Suppose I were to say I'm seeking a connection between Mother Crum, Judge Jeffries—and the gipsies."

"I'd say you were barking up the wrong tree."

"Suppose I were to say it's been suggested that the gipsies avoided Tabitha's house."

Jack laughed. "They used to be friends, Tabitha and Daniel's wife, Fleur. Had a falling-out. Some clash of power. Tabitha never believed in the Power herself; she humoured Fleur. But one day she called Fleur a silly one, Fleur suddenly became accident-prone, swore Tabitha was behind it, and that was it. From then on Crum Cottage was taboo. Fleur spread the word that no Smith was to go near or woe betide them. *That*, incidentally, is why Fleur is convinced that the family are innocent of Judge Jeffries's death. Put the Judge in Crum's? Never! Wouldn't have set foot! More than their life's worth!—" Jack mimicked. "The Power . . ."

"Would that apply after Tabitha had gone?"

"Oh yes. The Power would remain in her house. And far be it from us to mock."

The Pheasant was in sight, some welcoming lights already twinkling. A reminder that night wasn't so far distant. Pup was put on her lead; they would meet a car or two now.

"Fleur's law," Bassett said. "Is that a good-enough reason to cross the Smiths off a suspect list?" Jack, he thought, would know the strength of it.

But Jack shook his head. "Fleur forgets. A lot of the younger Smiths have been to school."

Yet Bassett himself would have been loath to enter the cottage of a wise-woman, *any* empty cottage, in the black of night. Deep down he knew he was as vulnerable as the next man.

"You said nothing has changed, Jack. Presumably you meant that alibis eighteen months ago still hold firm."

"The rest of the family were together on the night the Judge went missing. Family conference."

"That's a lot of alibis to crack." Bassett made it a statement; really it was a question. Jack understood.

"I know," he said, smiling. "The old story of gipsy people ganging up. But there was a legitimate reason. They were together to discuss an appeal for Aaron and Ike. Money, ways and means. They wanted a top lawyer, the best that money could buy. The money was there, pledges of more to come. Then—the Judge vanished."

And here came the reason why Jack believed, as did Daniel, that none of Daniel's people was responsible.

"Result? Appeal kyboshed. They couldn't find a lawyer who would take the case. Whoever *was* responsible for the Judge's disappearance effectively condemned Aaron and Ike to serve their sentences. And according to Dan"—Jack took on the old gipsy's gruff tone—"that weren't no Smith."

EIGHT

Saturday. There had been a frost overnight, cold nipped Bassett's fingers when he fed his chickens their mash and visiting wildlife some breakfast delicacies; but by half past eight the sun was out, the frost a glistening layer of moisture on the lawns. Bassett was convinced they had better weather in this part of the world than anywhere he had lived since his childhood in Hampshire. Or was it simply that being retired he had more time to notice good weather? Time and freedom. Freedom to choose whether to go out in bad weather or not. One of life's luxuries.

Since the weather wasn't bad he elected to go to town: to change his library books and drop in on Bob Greenaway.

It was a restful drive to Glevebourne. What little traffic there was consisted mainly of a fleet of Land-Rovers heading for a rally. Beautiful vehicles, Land-Rovers. Gave him a near-sensuous feeling, they looked so *right*, especially here, countryside in every direction. Might have himself a Land-Rover one day. Only he knew he never would, he liked the car he had, his Citroën. Liked the armchair comfort, the way it stayed level, ironed out bumps. He liked its looks. He liked it because it reminded him of Mary. She still travelled with him in the passenger seat, he talked to her as he always had, without turning his head; and now and then laughed and joked.

Anything that looks right usually *is* right, he might be saying to her now. Take Land-Rovers. This car. Any plane you can fly by the seat of your pants. Take Concorde. Take the ketch they had dreamed of sailing round the world once upon a time.

Crum Cottage never had looked right. Not the cottage itself, the contents. The body. Darn it, the whole thing, but the body in particular. It had nagged at him, allowed him no peace. Always there at the back of his mind: something wrong, something *not right.* An image of the body sitting in its armchair. Beseeching him. Look! Trying to get a message through his thick skull.

At last he knew what it was. He'd woken up this morning with the answer: the body was too *comfortable.*

For a second, contrarily, he felt reluctant to see Bob. It was one thing pandering to your own innate curiosity, another to rope yourself in. But it was too late, he had given his word: he had told Jack he would see what he could do for the Smiths.

How?

He stifled a sigh. Chuckled at something Jessie had said. "Get a punch on the nose, it take some of us a fortnight to fall down."

Says it all, Mary! Like Mother Crum, he would have been content to potter about his beloved country lanes if only the clues had been there. But a judge? Think judge and you thought city and pavements; you thought high-rise, impersonal, grey; and crime in capitals, if you'll pardon the expression.

You thought you'd left all that behind.

The chuckle restored Bassett's balance. There were no grey streets in Glevebourne, the highest structure was a church steeple, and Glevebourne Police Station was no supermarket for the dispensation of law but a solid, attractive Georgian building standing in its own grounds.

Entering, Bassett touched his hat to the desk sergeant, re-

ceived a thumbs-up, took the wide curved stairs two at a time—
for the first half-dozen—remarked the space, the light, the
small-town views of trees and sun-kissed buildings from the
windows; and almost envied Inspector Robert Greenaway his
place of work. A far cry from some of the offices he had oper-
ated out of. Out being the significant word.

"Good grief! You here?" he exclaimed, sticking his head
round Bob's door. Doors with coded locks hadn't arrived here
yet. "Catch me in on a day like this!"

"Catch you in any day when you were on the Force!"

"Ah, well. Stay in and they always knew where to find you."

That raised a grin. Bob was on the telephone, on hold by the
look of it. "Come in—" He beckoned, waved Bassett to a chair.
"Daren't let this go, I won't get through again." With his free
hand he pushed a Missing Person poster across the desk.
"That's why none of us recognized him. Had an aversion to
being photographed; the only decent likeness they could come
up with was this. Nothing like him, is it?" he said, as Bassett
looked and slid the poster back.

"No doubt about identification?"

None whatsoever. The body was indisputably that of Hugh
Jeffries.

"Hello?" Something was happening on the other end of the
line. Bassett politely averted his gaze, let it drift to Andy Miller's desk, cluttered, banished behind a filing-cabinet . . .
room made for a flower in a small glass jar; from an admiring
WPC? . . . and back to Bob, neat as ever, immaculate shirt-
sleeves, desk as tidy as the man: an interesting stack of files at
his elbow. "Thank you." Receiver replaced. Smile for Bassett.
"What's new?"

"Not a lot. Snippets. Might be useful."

"Such as?"

"Such as the gas fire. 'Tweren't Tabitha Crum's. She
wouldn't have had gas anywhere near, would have tainted her
medicines."

"Mm. Herbalist, wasn't she?" Bob Greenaway was not impressed. "Jeffries probably took it there himself."

"He had the key?"

"He had the key."

Which came as no surprise to Bassett; and made life easier for them, Bob Greenaway said, cut out a lot of whys. A bunch of Smiths had only to follow Hugh Jeffries.

"Mite dilatory of him to let them," Bassett murmured. In a cheerier voice, "Word is, Bob, the Smiths were all at a family gathering the night the Judge went missing. They were discussing an appeal for the two who—"

Bob Greenaway cut him short. "They've had eighteen months to think that one up."

"Word is, they told the same story at the time."

"Word is," Bob Greenaway mocked. "Whose word?" he asked slyly.

Bassett affected sheepishness. "I've been asked to do a spot of private investigating."

"I step back in astonishment!"

"Eh?"

"Knew you wouldn't be able to leave it alone! Ha!" Bob Greenaway snorted, but these two had a rapport. "OK," and a grin now, "what do you want to know?"

Bassett pushed his hat to the back of his head and crooked a finger towards the desk. "What you got?"

"Got the name of Crum Cottage's new owner."

A file was consulted. "Alan Damer-Preece, hyphenated. Works in Dubai. Seems he left the key with his old pal Hugh Jeffries, the cottage Hugh's for the use of. Knew nothing about the disappearance, hasn't been home for five years, never met Hugh's sister—so it follows that she would not have contacted him—and was in Dubai for the whole of the critical period. Chief spoke to him on the phone, put a few pointed questions: wasn't he concerned about his property, expect to hear news of it at any time? Seems Preece thought it OK as a gift but would not have touched it with a barge pole normally. From which we

assume he's well-heeled. He's only recently begun to appreciate its current potential market value. Couldn't recall what
furniture was in the cottage, so couldn't say if anything was
missing. Seems the small items were cleared out by Miss Crum
before she took herself off to a nursing home for her remaining
days. Sold to a bona fide dealer, whose name is here somewhere—"

"Not a Smith."

"No. A Mr. Lacey. Got that from your Mr. Arkwright."

Good. Saved Bassett the trouble: it was something he would
have had to check out.

"Jeffries's sister," he said. "Hadn't met Preece, you say. But
she knew about the cottage?"

"Says not. Says she can understand Hugh not sharing it with
her. He knew she'd want to take her deprived kids there for
holidays."

"*Five* years, and her brother never lets slip—?"

"Says not," repeated Bob Greenaway. "Says he knew she
wouldn't take no for an answer. She freely admits it. Crusader
type. Furious about houses standing empty *any*where while
people are being shoved into bed-and-breakfast accommoda-
tion. And believes passionately that every child should have the
opportunity to play on unpolluted grass once in a while."

"Social worker?"

"Does it for free."

Bassett's crowsfeet deepened. "Best believe her, then."

"We do," the other said. He looked up from a report he'd
been reading. "On paper Jeffries seems an ordinary chap.
Nothing against him. Bachelor. Forty-three—"

"Bachelor," Bassett said; a hint of meaning.

"Normal bloke," said Bob Greenaway. "Shy, loner, but had
girlfriends." Light stress on the girl. "One in particular about
ten years ago. His sister didn't meet her, they weren't that
close, but says Hugh was getting serious until something fouled
it up. In Chambers then, Bristol way. Casual girlfriends thereaf-

ter. Colleagues seem to confirm. He seldom spoke of his attachments—"

Bob broke off as Sergeant Miller breezed in carrying two mugs of coffee and a sandwich, and sighing laboriously, "Got trapped!" Andy's face lit up cheerfully when he saw Bassett. "Expected you yesterday, guvnor." He handed one coffee to Bob Greenaway, who looked overtly to see how much he'd spilt, put the sandwich on a corner of the desk, and gave the second coffee to Bassett. "I'll get me another."

"Nice of you, Andy."

"Andy!" Bob Greenaway barked as the sergeant made for the door. "Don't take all day this time," he said, the sting leaving his voice.

"Guv!"

"Loner with a girlfriend," Bassett muttered when Andy had gone. "Used the cottage as a love-nest."

"You're thinking, find the lady."

"Thinking discretion, Bob. Privacy. Secrecy. Thinking that so far I've found nobody who's seen Hugh Jeffries or a woman at the cottage. Implies a married woman."

"We thought about it," the other admitted. "Decided that if a woman had been involved in the death, even on a sideline, all traces of her having been in the cottage would have been removed."

Bassett said nothing.

"No point in my asking you who you're working for?"

Bassett shook his head. "Me and Sam Spade don't breach confidences."

Bob Greenaway shrugged inoffensively. "I have no choice. As Sherlock Holmes would have said: eliminate all other factors and the one which remains must be the truth. Wanda Jeffries and all known friends and colleagues of her brother's were eliminated first time round. Damer-Preece was in Dubai, he didn't fly home for Christmas—that was established by the Chief. Everything will have to be re-checked, but there's not much hope of turning up anything new. I'm left officially with the Smiths." Sorry.

"Interesting thing is, though," he continued, as he took a small screwtop jar of sugar out of a drawer, "they all have alibis for December 17th, the day the Judge disappeared, nothing for later dates. That could indicate that either they *know* he died on that date—or that they are, as they claim, innocent." He offered the sugar: no thank you. "They're not stupid. As time wore on they'd have had the intelligence to realize it was going to be well-nigh impossible to prove the *actual* date of Jeffries's death, yet they've prepared no additional cover."

Bassett regarded Bob thoughtfully. "Having second thoughts?"

"Let's say I'm beginning to wonder. But procedure is procedure." He threw a glance at the files, all to be gone through. "They are the reason I'm stuck in here." A pause. "One snag you might like to know about: the Smith family conference lasted from ten-ish on the Saturday morning to the early hours of Sunday. Jeffries left Hereford at roughly the same time, ten a.m. So it could have been an invention." He ended with an expressive shrug.

"What if it wasn't?" Bassett said quietly.

"Still difficult, officially. He could have been kidnapped. Taken and dumped in the cottage later."

The telephone rang. Bob Greenaway grimaced. "You're right, they know where to find you." The conversation was short. "Chief," he told Bassett. "But you stay and finish your coffee." He retrieved his jacket from its hanger, gazed at the files on his desk. "I ought to lock those up," he said slowly, fastening his jacket buttons. "On the other hand . . ." A flick of an eyebrow, and while he brushed himself down and neatened his cuffs: "We could be useful to one another.

"In the meantime I'll press on, Harry. You taught me the art —get 'em talking. Sniff out one lie, one mistake—"

If only it were that easy.

Yet occasionally . . . occasionally it was.

. . . .

Alone, Bassett reflected on the dead man that whispered; on the friend in Dubai; on the sister; and on Daniel Smith. Was it possible for Daniel to have been lied to by grandsons Aaron and Isaac, and/or other members of his family later? He had believed the police theory "Smiths threaten Judge, Judge dies, Smiths must have done it" too simple. But wasn't that family conference a shade *too convenient?*

Perhaps not. The Smiths were settled gipsies, had jobs to go to; a weekend would be the most favourable time for them to hold a get-together. Likewise for a gentleman to entertain his lady.

Rising, Bassett opened a file on Bob Greenaway's desk, examined the contents, found nothing new. Nothing appertaining to a girlfriend: seemingly no one had supplied a name. The post-mortem report?—a preliminary . . . His eyes touched Andy's sandwich. A feather-light touch, but oh! A second, and he was lifting a corner: beef, warm and juicy, a slice off the end of a roast. His gastric juices quickened. He turned away; put the file to one side, selected another. This related to the original crime, the crime against Rosie from Hereford. He lowered a buttock to the edge of his chair, his hat fell off . . . he read . . . scribbled down names, addresses, dates . . . read on . . . became absorbed. The smell of beef flirted with his nostrils.

Andy's returning startled him. "Not my day—!" The young sergeant pulled up in the middle of the office. "Where's Bob?"

"Summoned, Andy. Upstairs." Bassett was on his feet, patting files into their former positions, successfully concealing the desktop from Andy's view. "I can see you are busy," he said, massaging his nose as he moved towards the door. He hesitated when he was on a level with the young sergeant, patted him on the arm, holding his attention that bit longer.

"Jeffries's lady-friend, Andy. Goes once, twice, how many times? to Crum Cottage. Her lover disappears. Why didn't she tell the police where he might be?"

"At a guess she's married."

"So? What was to stop her from making an anonymous phone call? Put your thinking cap on. Leave you to it."

He was slinking out along the corridor when he heard Andy's bellow. His pace increased. Succumbed to a sin of the flesh, Mary! Couldn't help it, I'm only human!

At least he had the grace to feel embarrassed.

NINE

"What would have prevented the lady-friend from making an anonymous telephone call?" he muttered to himself as he crossed the police car park to fetch his library books from his car. "And who—where—is she?"

Books under his arm, he stood and debated anew. From here there were two routes to the library. He chose the old-town route, the route that would also take him past Jim McPherson's surgery.

An hour later he was home. He hadn't changed his library books, he'd forgotten to buy a crusty loaf from Home-Bake, oh! —and he'd lost his hat. But no matter: Doc had provided him with his first line of inquiry, something he could get his teeth into; and what was more he wouldn't have to stray far.

Doc had found nothing to conflict with the theory of a beating, he said in the beginning. No hidden bullet or stab wound. No existing game leg, old wound or injury, no detectable poison, drugs or organic disorder that might have contributed to Jeffries's death. Actual injuries were as previously stated: broken ribs, cracked patella, incomplete fractures here and there. Some internal bleeding, but if caught in time this would not have killed the man.

So what did kill him?

A depressed fracture. Doc had drawn the flat of his hand

across the forehead to demonstrate where. "I think a final finishing-off blow."

Meaning? That the forehead had already been damaged. Bruising indicated an earlier blow. How much earlier? Going on guesswork and nothing more, Doc calculated anything up to an hour.

It was emergencies only at the surgery on Saturdays, so Doc had been free to talk. They had sat in the peace of a cobbled garden, a section of an old stable-yard, where a horse trough had been converted to a table, seats had been fashioned from cut-down barrels, old wooden wheelbarrows overflowed with spring flowers, and the sun created patterns on an ancient stone wall.

"An hour. In other words and for argument's sake the Judge received a good hiding—then came a gap in time—then the fatal blow. He might have escaped, they caught up with him, and—?"

No. The first blow to the forehead might have been the first of a series, the death blow the last. With injuries like his, Doc said, Jeffries wasn't going anywhere. If he had tried, well, one lung was, say, pricked rather than pierced, but any uncontrolled movement . . . And there was also the leg.

"What about facial damage?" Bassett had asked.

None to speak of.

"No cracked jaw, loose teeth, broken nose?"

A slight nosebleed, no broken bones.

"Doesn't ring true, does it?" Bassett had said. "We say the man was beaten up. Right-o, picture that. They're angry—whoever they are. You're angry with me—you bop me on the chin or nose. As long as I stay on my feet you can't put the boot in. We say the boot was put in: therefore Jeffries must have ended up on the floor. Therefore—why no black eye, no split lip, no damage to the face?"

Why had there been nothing about the man to suggest a fight? He was too clean. He should have been mussed up. Blood, broken skin, *grazing* somewhere.

He died where? In his opinion, for what it was worth, Doc said, Jeffries died in that armchair. Want details? he asked. But details weren't necessary: the fact that Hugh Jeffries was sitting in the chair when found, sitting neatly, was what had bugged Bassett. He had eventually reasoned, and reasoned again with Doc, that if the man had suffered a beating and was then dumped he'd have been dumped on the floor or flung into the armchair. Attacked outside, in winter, there should have been supporting evidence—dirt, dead-leaf debris, cobweb. If indoors, there should be at least scuff marks on the carpet—and surely he would have been left finally where he lay? Instead, there he was, comparatively neat and tidy, sitting in an armchair as if he had died in his sleep.

As if somebody had taken pity on him? Nursed him? Looked after him when they saw they had gone too far?

How far had they intended to go, for heaven's sake?

Besides—the death blow. Sit him down, make him nice and comfortable, then finish him off? No. Think of that kneecap. Takes a deal of force to crack a kneecap. The act of a callous attacker. Callous one moment, *then* kind, then finish him off? Didn't ring true.

Weapons. After an interval of eighteen months Doc wouldn't hazard any guess as to what weapons had been used. What he could say, however, was that the fatal blow hadn't been struck with a hammer, iron bar, candlestick or blunt instrument of definite shape. The depression was irregular, no true definition.

Rock? Stone? Could be, yes.

That was when Bassett had said quietly, intensely, "Suppose all you had was a body, Jim. No foreknowledge. What else could have caused those injuries?"

The answer came. Car accident. If he had found the body in or near a crashed vehicle, Doc said, the injuries would almost have spoken for themselves: rib damage—steering-wheel in the chest; patella—knee violently striking the glove compartment or object protruding from it; the first blow to the forehead—

head in contact with a windscreen, a thump, need not have gone through.

But Doc wouldn't have been able to account for the death blow.

No matter. Country lane, misses a bend, hits a wall or a tree, is knocked senseless, recovers, opens the door, too dazed to realize the knee won't hold him, falls—his head hitting rock. "What say you, Jim?"

He'd collapse rather than fall, Doc said. Meaning that Jeffries was unlikely to have killed himself. And even if he had, how did his body get to the cottage?

Assume he had a passenger.

And now they were getting there. Jeffries hadn't hit his head fatally getting out of the car; he was alive when he got to the cottage. "The last blow, you said, Jim, came after a measurable gap in time. How much handling could he have taken before those ribs did pierce a lung?"

A fair amount as long as it was gentle.

Gentle. They had both winced. Gentle handling . . . followed by . . . No callous sustained attack with a little kindness thrown in; but a car accident, tenderness from the passenger, death at the hands of another. *That* fitted the picture in Bassett's head.

Jeffries must have been in the driving seat, Bassett mused now. His own car hadn't a scratch on it. So—that was what he had to find out first: since it wasn't his own car Hugh Jeffries was driving—whose car was it?

The woman's? The Judge was unmarried, wouldn't have mattered if he was seen with a female companion. Wouldn't have mattered greatly if *she* was married if, for example, he'd brought her from Hereford. Yet they seemed to have taken pains not to be seen. Implication?—that the lady must live, or feared recognition by someone who lived, in this area. Could have met her while he was walking. Comes for a visit, goes for a stroll, up pops the lady, they chat . . . Have to see if we can find her.

That trip to Crum Cottage first, however. How was he to get in? His own door was very like old Mother Crum's, and good coppers make good criminals! He weighed his own key in his hand. With a little bit of jiggling . . .

A fusty smell, the drag mark fainter, and studied with a slightly different speculative eye this time. Imagine a man injured but blessed with the will and reserve of energy to hop or be half-carried. Agony, yes, but men had suffered worse. For love of a woman, Bassett added unconsciously. Better still, assistance from two people, arms linked to form a cradle . . . carry him in, one leg dragging. Bassett followed an invisible trail to the sitting-room, went in—and promptly out again.

Why that drag mark on only one spot, just inside the hall? *Had* Jeffries been set upon at the door?

No. Bassett backtracked, went through the motions of bringing an injured man in and—of course! common sense!—the helper would have relaxed his or her hold on Jeffries in order to use the key. Also, it was night, had to be. There'd have been a torch beam to direct, wouldn't do the leg much good to bang it against walls or door jambs. An inevitable shifting of position then, one moment of clumsiness resulting in a short straight-forward drag mark. No hint of a struggle. No, no, the picture was of solicitude. Whoever helped Jeffries into the cottage was known to him, at any rate was someone he trusted. He, she, cared about him. Gently into the sitting-room, gently into the chair. He wasn't dumped. You don't *dump* the victim of a car crash.

So far, so good.

Gently to the armchair, made comfortable. Then what?

His companion—one person could have managed in desper-ate circumstances, nobody else around for example—Hugh Jeffries's companion would go to seek aid. Doctor. Ambulance . . . Why didn't they come?

Assume they weren't called.

Why not? What happened? What changed the situation?

Death?

Bassett surveyed the sitting-room. The Judge had been facing the door, would have seen who entered, murder in mind. Suppose—suppose the companion left, ostensibly to fetch help, but searched for a rock outside instead, waited until he closed his eyes, then came in . . .

Take some nerve. Dark, creepy, no street lighting. No lights from neighbouring houses. Which had, on reflection, been to the killer's benefit. As it had been to the lovers'.

Bassett's roving gaze rested on the poker. *Poker.* A wieldy log poker. Why go outside for a rock when the perfect weapon was not a step away? Was the poker here the first time he came? Yes. No blood, he had given no thought to a weapon, but he recollected seeing it. "Clean," or Bob would have taken it. Stood in a stand, in shadow. Was that why the murderer didn't use it? Because he didn't see it? *Didn't know it was there?*

That meant the killer hadn't been inside the cottage before. A stranger. Whoever helped Jeffries in was a friend, knew the cottage, knew he had a key. The one who killed him—?

Two people, anyhow. At least two people knew eighteen months ago that Hugh Jeffries was here. Both stayed silent.

The burnt paper in the grate had been raked. Bassett wondered if the police had found anything useful. A small tightly-rolled ball of charred tissue had been peeled open fractionally to reveal a whitish unburnt centre, like a chocolate cream. He bent down: what one copper rejected might be another's vital clue. He shook out his handkerchief, placed the charred ball onto it, gathered the handkerchief at the corners, put it into his pocket.

Straightening, he looked towards the windows, sunshine pouring in through one, a mere trickle of light flitting in through a gap in the curtains at the other.

He stood for a minute watching the light, then went to the closed curtains and pulled them open. With his eyes he drew a line from the armchair through the window to a spot in the lane . . . went to the other window, looked out. "Poor old lad," he whispered to the ghost of Jeffries. "I fear it was the car accident that killed you. Someone took advantage. If you hadn't been hurt at the wheel of a car the chances are you'd be alive today."

He closed the curtains, leaving them as he found them.

In the kitchen he noticed a fly-speck on the table where the key had been. Fresh fly-specks. The tiniest creature leaves behind evidence of its passing, disturbs something, if only dust. He himself had trodden on a leaf or two outside; the police had altered the ash in the grate. His thoughts changed direction momentarily as he tried to see in his mind's eye the kitchen gay with herbs, flowers, berries and seeds, bottles and coloured jars as in an old-time apothecary's. He would have enjoyed meeting Tabitha Crum—nice old lady by the sound of it. And there was nothing odd about what she did; his maternal grandmother used to make her own face creams and bath oils. He put a toe to the pedal-bin lever; bin empty now. He lifted the inner bin; nothing underneath.

He had left the door ajar. There was a leaf, dry and crinkly, behind it. There how long? Bassett automatically picked it up, put it in his wallet. From habit he looked where others often forgot to look: in that triangle between door and jamb, unseen when a door is open, where dust accumulates. A speck of red seemed at first to be a petal from an honesty flower. A second glance had Bassett brushing away grass seeds and dust with a fingertip. Not a petal, a fragment of red plastic. He placed it on a palm and flicked it over to inspect its underside; added it to the tissue in his handkerchief. Locked up. Went home.

Before setting out for Crum Cottage, Bassett had rung the police station and spoken to Ben Hacker, the desk sergeant. "Ben—do me a favour when you have a minute? Would you look in the Incident Book, please . . ."

The reply came shortly after he arrived home. No car accident had been reported in the Oakleigh Village area in December 1988.

Which didn't mean there hadn't been an accident. It simply meant that Bassett had to start his search entirely from scratch.

TEN

"Shall we?" No need to say *the* word, the tone of voice did it. Pup was already bouncing about, wagging her tail from the neck down.

Bassett combined pup's afternoon romp with his hunt for the site of a possible road accident. From a vantage-point on their favourite hill he focused on the immediate area spread out below like a relief map. From this height he could survey in seconds an area it would take days to investigate on foot.

He found the main Glevebourne Road, silver blobs, the flash of sun on windscreens, moving along it; traced the road as a line of trees curving along the valley, and up past Shooter's Hill in the near distance—where the road frequently filled with snow from hedgetop to hedgetop in winter—round to a dip between hills . . . up and over a rise . . . onto a winding course, dipping and rising . . . until it made its last turn at the big ash marking the junction, the junction with a lane that curved its way to the green and there became Long Lane.

Where Bassett lived, Tabitha Crum had once lived, and Hugh Jeffries had died.

The accident might have happened on the valley road, but Bassett didn't believe so. In his mind he had Jeffries being half-carried from the scene; the man would not have been carried any distance. It might have taken place at the bottom end of Long Lane, the other side of Crum's, but again he thought not. Assuming the car had hit a solid object and that the object was not another vehicle—if it had been, the accident would have been reported, surely—the object, he reasoned, must have been a wall or a tree. There weren't too many spots below Crum's where a driver might hit a tree.

So he looked for roadside trees from Crum's up; and as he also imagined the accident being cleared up swiftly, which

meant someone had to have telephoned for assistance in whisk-
ing the car away, he looked for a house with a telephone. In his
mind's eye he placed the cottages he couldn't see. There, Hillside. There, his own. There, Brown Owl Cottage. Then, walking to the hill's highest point, cottages he could see, a cluster of
doll's houses from this height, nestling round a tiny green.
From the green to Crum's was a mental distance of three seconds. On foot, he knew from experience, the journey took
three-quarters of an hour. An injured man and helper? It would
take ages to get from that tree to that tree, a blink of an eye
from up here.

Forget the cluster of cottages. Consider the others. Hillside
was a holiday cottage, and anyhow had no telephone. Keeper's,
no. He plumped for Brown Owl. He was going to guess that the
accident happened between Brown Owl Cottage and his own.
He'd examine that stretch first.

"Babydog! This way!" They made the descent.

A tiny listed cottage, Brown Owl, owned by a Mr. and Mrs.
Tipper. Mrs. Tipper had been born in the cottage. Her husband supplemented his pension by selling plants, cut flowers,
fruit in season. Their garden was permanently alive with colour.

Here also generosity. "Few geranium plants going spare, if
you'd like them," George Tipper said, while his wife made a
fuss of pup.

"Good of you, George!" Rabbits didn't eat geraniums, so the
gift was particularly pleasing. They talked geraniums for a
while; then: "Car accident round here about eighteen months
ago, George. Can't recollect it. Can you?" Bassett spoke as if he
ought to remember and was vaguely annoyed with himself
because he couldn't.

"That young fella who went into the gulley," George said
helpfully. "Won't have forgotten that?"

No. Cocky young townie, using the lane as a racetrack. Mary
had bandaged his cuts, given him a cup of tea, driven him
home, and not so much as a thank-you.

"We don't see many accidents round here . . ." None that wasn't talked about for days, anyhow. Bassett was told of some that had occurred over the years, none the one he wanted.

"No, we don't have many accidents," murmured Pamela Tipper. She often came in late. "Nor deaths—" Looking anywhere but at Bassett. "That poor Mr. Jeffries! People don't die very often round here, do they, George?"

"No, love. Once is usually enough."

Bassett hid a smile.

"This would have been wintertime," he persevered gently. "Christmas before last. Late one night . . ."

"Oh!" A squeak. "George! Remember that woman who came to use the phone?"

"No," replied George, preoccupied. He was busy with his plants.

"Said she'd broken down," his wife prompted. But George shook his head; it meant nothing to him.

"He'll remember in a minute," she told Bassett. "All out of breath she was, shook up. George offered her a cuppa—you must remember that, George!—but she wouldn't stop. Made her call and went."

"What was she like?" Bassett inquired.

Her perfume was what Mrs. Tipper remembered most. "It lingered in the house for days! I wish I knew what it was," she said wistfully. "What did she look like? Didn't see much of her, she was in too much of a state to be over-friendly. A bit aloof. Lovely hooded coat she had on, black, furry, must have cost a fortune. Have I said that—looked as if she had money? A lady, she was. Long coat. Might have been an evening cloak, like you see on the films. Red dress underneath. Gloves—"

From George: "And she was blonde."

"See? He does remember!" Giving a backward nod. "Trust a man to notice that. *Was* she blonde, George?"

"Blonde," George said, winking behind her back.

His wife, arms on top of the garden gate, screwed her head round to watch him counting out plants, then turned once more to Bassett. "Blonde," she said. George said blonde, blonde it was.

"Do you know who she telephoned, Mrs. Tipper?"

"A garage." She dug into her memory. "Yes! Funny how things come back to you. I asked if she wanted to look up a number, it was gone midnight, would there be a garage open, but she said she had an emergency number. Yes, it's all coming back. She made the call—no, I didn't hear what she said, I'm afraid—told us they were coming out, and said she'd get back to warn other vehicles. I nearly said what vehicles, no traffic here this time of night, but away she went, wouldn't hang on out of the cold. Or let George go with her. Went that way, towards your house."

"Did you see the car?"

No. "George came with her to the gate, but he didn't see it, it was further down."

"Did you by any chance see the breakdown truck?" The name on the side. Fingers crossed.

"We heard it. Oh, must have been a good twenty minutes later. That'll be it, George said, we can go to bed now. We'd been about to go up when the woman came, held on in case the garage let her down."

"That's not quite right, love." George looked up from what he was doing. Then to Bassett: "I came out once or twice, wasn't happy about a woman out on her own, seemed a mite heartless to leave her to it, that hour of night. Strolled down the lane in the end, saw a car drawing up by her car, so I came back. I can't tell you any more than that though, I only saw the lights." To his wife: "That's when I came in and said we could get off to bed now."

"I thought we heard a breakdown truck?"

"We did. A diesel of some kind, anyway. That was later on. We heard it go past when we were in bed."

Mrs. Tipper nodded. "He's right, you know. And that would explain it, wouldn't it?" she said to Bassett. "A breakdown truck in the middle of the night, some people would automatically think 'accident.' "

"I wonder," Bassett said. "You don't keep a diary, do you? Couldn't give me a rough idea when it was?" He smiled, head on one side: too much to ask?

"Can give you the date," George said. "Day before the Carol Service," he told his wife when she looked at him askance. "You were making a blouse."

"I was . . . Yes." She dug into her memory again. "I was. That's why we were still up! I thought people'd be sick of seeing me in the same old thing. I was all behind with it, so it must have been close to the day—"

"The day before," said George with a sort of practised casual air. "You were going on about the buttons." Driving him daft, frankly. "Those you had weren't fancy enough, but you couldn't change them because the next day was a Sunday."

"I took some off an old blouse in the finish. Fancy you remembering that, George!" Warmly.

George beamed. "I do take an interest in you, see?" To Bassett, devilishly: "And she was blonde."

Mrs. Tipper fetched her old calendars, which she saved for the pictures on them. The relevant calendar had the date of the Carol Service ringed: Sunday, December 18th. The night the blonde woman's car "broke down" was therefore Saturday the 17th.

The same Saturday that Hugh Jeffries had left Hereford and disappeared.

And Bassett had more than one reason to feel quietly excited. He had already examined the partly-burnt tissue he had retrieved from the grate in Crum Cottage. On one leaf, lipstick. On another, eye shadow. Blue eye shadow. And any man who has lived on this earth for any length of time knows that blue eye shadow usually complements blonde hair.

He found it. The tree. Another big ash, this one with a bare patch, bark missing from the trunk. Close inspection revealed

that the bare patch was splintered: an old wound, dry, dis-
coloured grey; and so manifestly the result of a good hard clout
it would have kindled a deal of speculation had the clout occurred in summer: something bashed into the ash down the
lane, by the looks of it! In winter people weren't always so
observant, in the week running up to a Christmas they had
more to do than go walking for the sake of it; and the snowfall
three days later would have camouflaged flattened foliage
round the base of the tree. By the time the snow thawed people
would have forgotten. Ash heals quickly anyhow.

With these thoughts Bassett was trying to convince himself.
But even without the sliver of paint embedded in the scar he
was fairly confident he was on the right track: the sliver of paint
clinched it. Gently he dug the flake out with his penknife blade
—it was brittle, ready to disintegrate at a touch—and studied it.
Glossy metallic on one side, laminated, all sections of paint:
primer, undercoat, top paint. Like layers of paper off a wall.
The flake had been knocked off the bare metal of a vehicle. He
put the flake carefully into one of the envelopes he'd brought
for the purpose. Poking around the base of the tree, disturbing
new shoots but not many, there was sandy soil here and an
abandoned ants' nest, he unearthed pieces of amber plastic,
recognizably from an indicator lens; headlamp glass and more
paint chippings. Might be coincidence, of course; might have
been a farm vehicle that bashed the tree. He would soon find
out.

Back home, he prepared a bundle of envelopes, large and
small, and then telephoned Bob Greenaway.

"Bob, I've something for you. For the lab. Pieces of what I
think might be evidence. All right if I bring them down?"

"You'll be lucky," the inspector said gloomily. "We are off
the case. County big guns have taken it over."

ELEVEN

"That summons to the top floor while you were here?" Bob Greenaway said. "That was it. To tell me that County wanted it, it was their baby. Didn't get far with the disappearance; it'll be interesting to see how far they get with this."

"We're damned annoyed about it." This from Andy.

Doc also was upset. "Pinched the body from me."

All three, Bassett making a fourth, had assembled in the Talbot in town. Not exactly a council of war, but it came close. If Bassett did have something, they would be more than delighted to beat the county bods at their own game.

"Think we're thick," Andy moaned. "When Bob asked one of them what they wanted us to do they said we could go back to issuing pig permits."

"I don't think they were very pleased with us," Bob said, a thin smile on his lips. "Reckoned we should have called them in from the word go."

"Cars every which way in the lane as I came out," Bassett said. "What leads are they following up, do you know?"

"I think they still fancy the Smiths."

"They don't know about the accident theory?"

Doc answered that one. "I'd put nothing in writing. And it *is* only a theory. I deal in facts. They'll have their own bloke on it now, in any case. Over to him."

"What *have* you got, guvnor?" Andy asked Bassett.

"A blonde who rang up for a breakdown service on the night the Judge disappeared. A blonde in the cottage. And bits from a car that bashed a tree."

The others weren't too enthusiastic. Wasn't Bassett doing the unforgivable?—making evidence fit a theory.

But what had they to lose? Bassett was independent, he had every right to investigate if he so wished. If he came up with the right answer, all to the good. "I'm game if you are," Greenaway said. "You can give me that parcel for a start. What do you want to know?"

"I want to know what car. Simple as that."

"As good as done. Give me two days."

Had Bassett been investigating officially he would have been delving into Hugh Jeffries's background in the interim. The victim's character often held a clue to why he or she had been murdered, and in turn to who did it. Often, not always. In this case he was hamstrung. To seek out Wanda Jeffries, the Judge's friends, colleagues, associates, might be to tread on police toes . . . Rosie, the lady from Hereford— he had passed on his notes to Jack, and wondered how Jack was getting on. Might it not have been advisable to wait? Even those who had felt kindly towards Aaron and Ike Smith might no longer do so now that the Judge had turned up dead. No smoke without fire, they might say. As Sally had, more or less. "Never really believed it of the Smiths . . . but now, it's different again, isn't it?" Ergo: it must have been them.

It must have been Aaron and Isaac who stole Rosie's porcelain. It must have been other members of the Smith family who did for the Judge.

Bassett held on to his own belief that the Judge was a victim of what the French call a crime of passion. A judge and a lady. And a jealous or angry third person: a husband or lover.

He did once consider: a gipsy and a lady? Yes? But only wild speculation could link in the Judge. A gipsy, a lady, and a judge? No, no. Notion rejected.

By Monday morning Bassett had decided to pursue a single trail: his original idea of starting from scratch. Which meant keeping in mind what he himself had seen of the body and the cottage, and waiting patiently for the results of the laboratory tests.

The results arrived late on Tuesday.

"Vauxhall Carlton, Saxon bronze!" Bob Greenaway announced cheerfully on the telephone. "Fairly new."

"Good grief!" Bassett said happily. "Registration number?"

Bob laughed. "Can't even give you the exact year. Paint analysis pinpointed that particular batch, but the car could have been produced in '87, sold in '88. Got me?"

"Got you."

"What's your next move?"

"Find a body shop. Quickest way I know of obtaining the name of this area's insurance assessor."

"What makes you so sure the car is from this area?"

"Instinct tells me that the lady lives locally. I'm guessing the car was hers. Unless she could afford to scrap the thing she must have had it repaired."

"Good luck," Bob said. "Don't forget—anything I can do, shout. But don't tell me anything—I'm duty bound to pass it on. Save it till you've got something concrete, then we'll take it from there."

TWELVE

Taylor's Body Shop—"First-Class Body Repairs and Respraying"—was in a disused quarry a mile from Glevebourne.

Bassett parked on gravel a cautious distance from a row of bashed vehicles and headed for the hangar-like shed comparable to many workshops on new Trading Estates. This one had an entire side opened up for ventilation. At one end a youth in overalls and plastic apron, goggles and mask hanging loose round his neck, was stripping masking material from a car recently treated to an all-over sky-blue facelift.

"Mr. Taylor?" Bassett shouted to the youth above the din of assaulted metal.

The youth threw a look to where at the other end of the

workshop a man was banging a wing of a silver-grey Ford with a dolly and leather mallet.

"No rush," Bassett called as he approached the Ford, wiry Reg Taylor having paused when he saw him nearing. Taking Bassett at his word, Reg gave the metal a few more healthy belts, groaned when cakes of mud avalanched from the under-side of the wing onto his paint-stained boots of many colours, and straightened. "Farmers! Bring half a field in with them." A further token bash, a run of a fingertip over the metal, and Reg laid down his tools.

"That was an expert's touch if ever I saw one," Bassett said genially.

The other accepted the praise with a modest smile. He had a frosting of paint on his nostril hairs, and a pallor which denoted a long association with paint fumes and cleaning fluids. "Won't keep you. Name's Bassett. Wonder if you can help me—"

"Ooh!" Reg drew in an expensive-sounding sharp intake of breath. "Up to me ears!"

"Not bodywork," Bassett said. "Wondered if you could give me the name of an insurance assessor or two."

Reg wiped his hands on a rag and thought for a second. "Les Palmer. He's the top man around here. There are some others, but Les is the main one in this area." He threw the rag down. "Want his phone number?"

Bassett followed him across to a workbench which had an office corner and a one-man filing system: invoices, receipts, work sheets and so on, varying from the pristine clean in spring-clips full to bursting to the grubby curly brown hanging from a row of nails. Ignoring these, Reg went to a display of business cards pinned to a fibre-board—everything from Chinese Take-Aways to Hand-Made Shoes.

He pointed. "That's Les."

Les Palmer, I.Mech.E., and an address in Priory Morton.

Priory Morton isn't so much a village as a village green. Every green is unique, varying in size from the pocket handkerchief at the top of Long Lane to something like this: many acres of commonland, sheep everywhere, dabs of different coloured paint on their backs, the marks of a variety of owners. Like oases in a desert, isolated clumps of trees denoted here a form, there a house or a cottage.

He stopped at the bottom of a drive up to a farm. He now had his bearings. The last time he passed here there had been mountains of apples in the yard at the top of the drive, and truckloads of apples destined for cider-makers trundling along the roads criss-crossing the common. The cycle had re-started: today apple blossom caught the eye.

Greenery of the exotic variety shielded Les Palmer's bungalow from view. All Bassett could see of it as he drew up outside the double wrought-iron gates was a conservatory and steps down to a lawn, where a toddler was playing ball with Grandma. Les Palmer's office was just inside the gates, an attractive chalet-style building that without the sign might have been mistaken for a summer-house.

A young woman in jeans and summer sweater came to meet him. "Are you the gentleman who phoned? Les won't be a minute. Would you like to wait in here?"

An office cum hobby-room. Model aircraft . . . Gave Bassett a twinge of nostalgia.

"Welcome to the dog-house!" Les Palmer. Gangling, balding, cheerful. He wore an open-necked shirt, a sleeveless Fair Isle pullover, and smelt faintly of glue. "Used to work from the house, but my wife talked me into building this. Too much underfoot, blasted nuisance on the quiet, and cost her a fortune in coffee."

Bassett laughed with him. "Built it yourself?"

"With a little help from friends."

"Very nice," Bassett said sincerely. "Been admiring your models. Learnt to fly in that one." A Harvard. He tore his eyes away. "Name's Bassett. I'm inquiring into an accident that happened about eighteen months ago."

"Police?"

"I'm assisting the police." It was true.

"Hit and run? Getaway vehicle? Or shouldn't I ask?" the assessor said as he produced something he referred to as his bill book.

"Elimination mainly, Mr. Palmer. Eliminate the cars we don't want, hopefully we'll find the one we do. Car's a Vauxhall. Vauxhall Carlton. Saxon bronze."

"Vauxhall Carlton. Don't see too many of them. I do recollect one. Here we are. Yes, Christmas week, 1988. Would that be it?"

"Sounds promising." Bassett returned the smile.

The assessor checked his book. "Insurance company notified me of a possible write-off on Tuesday the 20th. I went to inspect the car on the 30th." A re-check. "Yes. Christmas intervened. Inspected it at Davis's Garage. Do you know it? Garage and Car Hire."

"It rings a bell." Sally's granddaughter worked there. "Davis did the recovery?"

A nod. "It was his own car, out on hire. Hired it to some woman as a favour, and she promptly wrecked it."

Ah! Bassett gestured. "Wouldn't have the woman's name, would you?"

Sorry, no. "All I need to know is the car, registration number, and where to go to inspect it."

"What's the procedure?" Bassett said. "A claim goes to the insurance company, they notify an assessor, say you, you inspect the vehicle. What happens next?"

"I check damage against repair estimate, if there is one, report back with or without recommendations. They take over from there."

"I see. Your job's done. You're a freelance? You bill them for services rendered." Hence the bill book. "May I make a note of those details?" He took out his notebook and pen, said thank you when Les Palmer handed him the book. "How'd you

know the car was hired by a woman?" he asked conversationally.

"Garage chat," was the amused reply. "The customary dis-
paraging remarks about lady drivers. She rolled it."

Bassett commiserated, with the lady. "The chat didn't extend
to who she was? No. Unethical," he agreed. "Not to worry." He
made notes. "I don't suppose you can recall where it happened?"

Another negative. "They probably did tell me, but I see so
many." The assessor looked away thoughtfully, as if raking his
memory. Bassett watched him. Garage owner and insurance
assessor just might meet socially and, ethics or not, just might
have conversed about the night the garage owner hired out his
very own car to a lady . . . But there was nothing evasive in
the other's manner, nothing contrived about the small frown of
concentration. Which cleared as he smiled an apology. "No.
Can't be sure."

Anyhow, the insurance company would have a sketch-map.

Bassett nodded. "The exact location, of course. You don't
have to inspect the scene of the accident . . . ?"

Insurance companies seldom bothered, Les Palmer said.
Their sole interest was the claim against them, while his was the
damage to the vehicle. Both were keen to keep costs down,
which included his fees. They would increase if he had to inspect every accident scene.

"Cost-cutting everywhere!" Bassett said, smiling. "The insurance company's main concern is the cost in putting a vehicle
right, your job is to ensure they are not taken for a ride, if you'll
pardon the expression. Is that what you're saying? Meet with
much fiddling?"

"Some. Cheek more than fiddling. Rust and worn parts, for
instance. My report points out wear, the client may then be
requested to pay a proportion of the cost of improvement.
You'd be surprised how many people think they can get all their
repairs done on the strength of a minor bump."

Bassett grinned. "Can't blame them for trying. Any query on this claim, the Carlton?"

None. "Straightforward all through. No police involved. No counter-claim. Damage assessed, write-off recommended. QED."

"No complications."

"Absolutely. Nigel Davis had all the gen—accident claim form with sketch-map, everything required. I sent in my report, in due course he got his cheque."

"Could be I have the wrong vehicle," Bassett said. "I thank you for your time, Mr. Palmer. Big help."

"Another one eliminated?"

"Well . . ." Bassett said noncommittally.

He left and headed for Davis's Garage.

"I'm afraid Mr. Davis isn't here at the moment," the girl said brightly. "He won't be long, though. Ten minutes?"

"May I wait?" She nodded, wide-eyed, and went to serve petrol to a customer. An unaffected young lady: fair hair tied in a pony tail, intelligent face, and a healthy fresh-scrubbed appearance.

"You're Julie," he said when the customer drove off.

"Yes!" She gave a pleased laugh. "Do I—?" A hand moved to the neat white collar at her neck. "Oh-h . . ." She groaned and laughed again. "You're Detective Chief Superintendent Bassett."

"As was," Bassett said, and they both laughed. "It was you who taught your gran that mouthful."

"Guilty! And you've come to ask me questions!" she protested. "And me looking like this!"

"Nothing wrong with how you look. But I don't want to question you. What I'd like is a peep at the firm's car-hire book."

"Mr. Davis shouldn't be long," Julie said, throwing a glance behind her. "He's popped home. I think Heather—Mrs. Davis

—must be off-colour. He's been going home a lot during the day lately."

"Is that the Davis house?"

Julie followed Bassett's gaze. "No, that's Stan's. The Davises live opposite—the big house. See it through the trees?"

"The Chestnuts—" Bassett read from the developer's board. "New housing estate?"

"Mm. All but those two. Lovely houses," Julie enthused, not without envy. "Stan reckons he feels like Pa Kettle, his little cottage next door to those posh houses. He keeps talking about moving to a flat now that he's on his own, but I don't think he will, he's too fond of his garden, never out of it. And let's be honest, these places are a dream, but they don't give you much to dig a spade into."

"Stan's a widower? . . . His wife has left him," Bassett said, when Julie gave him a certain look.

"About eighteen months ago."

"Oh." Sympathy.

"I'm not sure that she's *left* him *exactly*. Mrs. Davis says she phones Stan once in a while. She's *working* away. In Bristol. Or Bath. Not sure which."

"Which one is Stan?" Bassett said mock-sheepishly.

"There, in the shop. No—he's in the showroom. He's Mr. Davis's right-hand man, been with him since he left school. Mr. Davis, Mrs. Davis, Stan—they were friends when they were little. Mrs. Davis once told me she nearly married Stan . . . He's nice, but he's always been the poor relation. Mr. Davis has always been well-off. This garage was his father's." Julie glanced up and down the road, all quiet now. No sign of her boss. "I don't have anything to do with the car-hire side, Mr. and Mrs. Davis deal with that. But I don't see why I shouldn't show you the book—"

The telephone rang as they entered the office. Julie answered it. "Davis's . . . Oh, hello, Mr. Jay . . . Hold on, I'll go and ask him." She signalled towards a desk diary marked Car-Hire on her way out . . . "Stan—when will Mr. Jay's car be ready?"

She returned in a flash. "An hour, Mr. Jay . . . You're welcome. 'Bye."

The desk diary was ruled to accommodate hire-car numbers and model, customer, time vehicle out, returned, and margin space for any comments. But it was the current book.

"Do you think I could have the book for the last two years?" Bassett begged.

"This cupboard, I think," Julie said. "Yes, here we are. Last year and the year before."

Bassett turned to the relevant date: Saturday, December 17th. But his attention was caught and held by the entry for the 18th . . . On Sunday, December 18th, the Vauxhall Carlton, Mr. Davis's own car, registration number corresponding to that supplied by Les Palmer, had been hired to a Mrs. Abbott. In the comments margin: "Write-off. See accident claim."

Mrs. Abbott. Lady driver. *Sunday.*

Bassett wanted the accident to have taken place on the Saturday.

On Saturday the 17th the same car, entry squashed in beneath other hire-cars, had been booked to a Jeffries—and then cancelled.

"How long have you worked here, Julie?"

"Just over twelve months."

"You won't be able to clarify this entry, then. No matter."

Bassett wrote details of both entries in his notebook. "Do you have a customer address file?" he asked.

They did. Bassett checked: no Hugh Jeffries on file.

He gave Julie the books. "Thank you."

"You're welcome." She went with him onto the forecourt. "You must come and have tea with me," Bassett said. "Next week, perhaps."

She nodded, wide-eyed and shy. "Thank you." Her chin went up. "Here's Mr. Davis."

"I won't stop now," Bassett said. "I'll come another day."

He drove the hundred yards to the Davises' house. A woman, a strikingly pretty woman in cool ice green, was in the garden, strolling on the lawn, lost in a daydream, it seemed to Bassett. He didn't go to speak to her. What had he to say?

She wasn't blonde. Her hair was chestnut brown.

He drove home thinking of Stan's wife.

THIRTEEN

Thursday dawned drizzly and remained overcast all day, but the wet dried up for Bassett's visit to the insurance company. "Ask for Mr. Dorridge," assessor Les Palmer had advised. "He's the man I deal with. Gloucester Office."

Gloucester. Charming city. Flower-sellers on the pavements. A fiddler playing a catchy tune. Fountains in the square.

On an impulse Bassett bought a bunch of tulips for Mrs. Fielding, Mr. Dorridge's secretary, with whom he had spent a good ten minutes on the telephone. She had been extremely pleasant and accommodating. Mr. Dorridge wouldn't be available for some days, but she would be able to supply the information he sought.

Modern offices in an old well-preserved building: all open plan, potted plants and radiators. Black-haired Mrs. Fielding as attractive as her telephone voice, with a brisk efficient manner which had escaped the abrasiveness that affected so many women nowadays.

"For you . . ." The flowers. From Jo Fielding genuine delight. "How lovely of you!" She completely forgot to ask for a peep at his "authority." "It's all here ready. Vauxhall belonging to Mr. Davis. Car classed as a write-off. Meaning cost of repairs would have exceeded list value of the car. Cheque to Mr. Davis. Everybody satisfied."

Until now.

Bassett studied the paperwork set before him: the proposal form for insurance for the hire period, cover-note book, accident claim form submitted by Davis, with its sketch-map of where the accident took place . . . Studied and stifled a sigh.

He had hoped that the entry for Mrs. Abbott in Davis's hire-book had been written in the Sunday column because no room had been left under Saturday. But here it was. The proposal form and cover-note copy proved that the car *had* been hired by Mrs. Abbott on the Sunday. December 18th. If it were to fit in with Bassett's theory that Mrs. Abbott was the woman who had telephoned for a breakdown service, that date should have been the 17th, the Saturday.

The place was wrong, too. This accident hadn't taken place in Long Lane, Oakleigh. According to the sketch-map, it had happened three miles away, on the main country road between Oakleigh and a neighbouring village, Lymock.

The date and the site of the accident were both wrong.

Yet the car appeared to fit.

"Is it possible that someone made a mistake with the date . . . ?"

Jo Fielding shook her head. "Very unlikely. Cover-notes are numbered, they must be used in sequence. May I?" She received the cover-note book from Bassett. She had pinned the book open at the required page. Now she removed the paper clip and flicked through the pages. "There, you see. Date order, time order. Different cars, of course. I think Mr. Davis has three hire cars."

"But this was his own—personal—car, I believe."

"You're thinking it should have been on garage cover?" Jo Fielding put her own interpretation on Bassett's query. "The garage does have bulk insurance, naturally. Any vehicle they have, any vehicle on their premises, is automatically covered by the garage policy. But this claim had to be treated separately because the car was out on hire."

"The hirer takes out his own insurance cover?"

"Oh yes." Jo Fielding explained the procedure. "The hirer—in this instance a Mrs. Alison Abbott from Abbott's Brook Farm —signs a proposal form, is given a cover-note, pays a premium, and is thereby insured independently and fully comprehensively for the duration of the hire. But only for the duration of the hire."

"Who makes out the cover-note?" Bassett asked. "The garage or hire firm, presumably."

"They act as our agents, yes."

"And the paperwork is done *before* the car is driven away?" Essential. Otherwise the car isn't fully insured.

"So," Bassett said, "I hire a car, complete and sign a proposal form, name, address, et cetera. I pay a fee for insurance cover, am given a cover-note. I have an accident, contact a garage . . ." Or, he mused on in silence, I move the car to a different spot, fake an accident, *then* telephone the garage. The woman's address: Abbott's Brook Farm. *Farm.* Land-Rover. Tractor. A diesel; we heard a diesel (engine), George Tipper had said. Needn't have been a breakdown truck; could have been a farm vehicle, doing the shifting.

Only one problem: the blonde telephoned for a breakdown service on the *Saturday* night; Mrs. Abbott didn't hire the Vauxhall until the Sunday.

"Mr. Davis didn't have *two* Vauxhall Carltons, did he, Mrs. Fielding? One for himself, one for his wife." Bassett made light of it.

"No." She made a face. "Trouble?"

Bassett smiled, a little wearily, Jo Fielding thought. "To be honest," he said, "the accident I'm chasing occurred the day before, on Saturday the 17th. I'm beginning to think I may have made a mistake."

He indicated the cover-note book. "These are sent in when they're all used up, I take it."

"Yes. Although fees and proposal forms are checked against them every ten days or so, either by a representative or when Mr. Davis brings dues to the office himself. Which he does occasionally."

Scant chance of forgery then, was Bassett's thought.

Jo Fielding picked up the book, began to flick through the

pages again. Suddenly: "How very odd . . . Somebody *was* going to hire that same car on the Saturday . . . Look. Cover-note for the 17th. Made out for the Carlton for a twenty-four-hour hire from eleven a.m. on the 17th—then cancelled. See?"

She showed Bassett the top copy stapled to its bottom copy in the book. "It happens," she continued. "A client books a car, fails to turn up, or has no valid driving licence or something stupid. We'll only accept a cancellation as a cancellation if the top copy is sent back."

"Why is that?"

"Because anyone could write cancelled and, as long as the car was returned in good order, pocket the fee. The top copy proves the car never went out."

Bassett nodded intelligently. "This cancelled top copy was originally torn from the book. I'd have thought it would remain in a book until the client collected the car."

"The garage might have been asked to deliver. They would take the paperwork—the top copy—with them. I'd say that's what happened here. It's been folded, as you can see."

"We don't know who the would-be hirer was?"

"*We* don't," Mrs. Fielding acknowledged. "Our cover-notes only carry car and hire details. The client's name would have been on the proposal form, but unfortunately they aren't numbered, so the one to go with this would've been scrapped. Mr. Davis should be able to tell you. He is bound to have it down somewhere."

Oh, he has! A cancelled booking for a Mr. Jeffries.

Which Mr. Jeffries? That was the question.

"Suppose," Bassett began slowly, "suppose the car *was* delivered, *was* accepted by the hirer, *was* driven on the Saturday . . . and when the car was returned the top copy cover-note was in the glove box . . . ?"

"There you have it, Mr. Bassett. That also goes on, we feel sure. There'd be nothing to prevent the garage from pinning the top copy back into the book, scrapping the proposal form, and, as I said, pocketing the fee. Nice bit of tax-free pocket money."

"For the garage owner."

"Or someone who works there. But the car would have to be returned intact. I thought you were looking for an accident?" Jo Fielding observed with some perplexity.

"I am, Mrs. Fielding, I am!" His flagging good humour was on the mend. He gave her one of his best smiles. "Your records. Proposal forms in particular. Might I beg a look at those sent in by Mr. Davis during the year prior to this accident?"

"No problem." She really was very obliging. "I can't show you the actual forms, they've been transferred to film."

"Meaning I can view them on a screen. Do nicely."

Jo Fielding unlocked a wall cupboard, selected a tape, fed it to a machine. "This goes back three years. I'll start you off and leave you to it while I put your flowers in water. They are lovely. I'm so grateful."

Bassett had no great affection for modern technology, albeit he had immense respect for the brains that invented and developed computers. But he took pleasure in playing with this toy. He was searching for a name. Jeffries. Or Abbott. If he could find a previous proposal form for Jeffries he'd have an address. He was sure the Jeffries who had booked a car from Davis's on December 17th was Judge Jeffries, but . . . Always a but.

A perky young lady with fashionable spiky hair and American-footballer shoulder-pads daintied in to inquire chirpily if he would prefer tea or coffee—?

"Tea would be very welcome, thank you."

—and daintied out again.

She brought him luck. He found Jeffries. A Hugh A. Jeffries, occupation lawyer, with an address at Bath, had signed a proposal form, that is, had hired a car from the garage on several occasions prior to the date of the accident; and if he had hired a car previously it was reasonable to assume that he and not an unknown Jeffries had hired, or at any rate had booked, a hire car on the 17th.

Bassett found no other Jeffries. Nor had Mrs. Abbott hired
before. But never mind: Bassett had a definite link between
Davis's Garage and the dead Judge.

Copies? Certainly, Jo Fielding said, when she came back with
two cups of tea. "Show me which you want. Did you find the
other accident?"

"Afraid not. I'm curious," Bassett said, smiling. "Everything
seems to be so *in order,* your system, I mean, excellent. The
hirer—say Mrs. Abbott—would you have sent someone to see
her, would she have had to sign, say, a declaration of truth,
anything like that?"

"Oh no." She answered his seemingly casual inquiry in like
vein. "As I think I said, Mr. Davis acts as agent. He would have
dealt with Mrs. Abbott, got her to fill the claim form in. She
would have signed that, of course, but the claim came in
through him. He made a thorough job of it as I recall. But then
he would, wouldn't he?" she said with feeling. "His own car."

His own car. The words echoed in Bassett's head. At last they
were beginning to make an impression. *His own car.* And he,
Nigel Davis, submitted the accident claim.

A moment or two to reflect. Then Bassett moved on.

He had found the car, *a* car which might fit the bill, had
followed it through, so to speak, until it was a wreck. What
happened to it then?

"Curiosity again, Mrs. Fielding. Nothing to do with my inquiry. Once you've paid out for a write-off a wreck becomes
insurance company property. Am I right? How do you dispose
of them? All these lumps of metal."

"We sell them, to a salvage firm if we can. Naturally we want
to recoup some of our losses. We notify a breaker, he goes to
see the wreck, we agree a figure, which more often than not is
determined by the breaker." She smiled. "Depends on how
much of the vehicle he can use. And we sell. Mr. Davis's car
would have gone to the major breaker in his area. Smith's Auto-
Salvage . . . I'll just organize these copies for you . . ."

"Smith's Auto-Salvage, did you say?" Bassett took up where they had left off when Jo Fielding sat down again.

"Proprietors Daniel and Mordecai Smith," she said. "I do so love those names. Daniel and Mordecai Smith. They have a certain dignity, don't you think?"

"Indeed they do. And you notify them, you say. They don't approach you?"

"We have agreements with salvage firms. We inform them of the wreck, tell them where it is, and so on. For example, there are two breakers in Mr. Davis's area. Holt's take lower-priced vehicles and rubbish. Smith's have first refusal on higher-priced late-model vehicles."

"The Vauxhall Carlton then would almost certainly have been offered to Smith's Auto-Salvage . . ."

"Oh yes," Jo Fielding said. "They would have had, as I said, first refusal."

Exit collusion. Exit for the moment any notion that included the Smiths helping someone at Davis's get rid of a car that might have been evidence.

"Was there—is there anything wrong with the claim?" Jo Fielding said tentatively. He hadn't mentioned fraud, but there was *some*thing . . .

"No, no, no." Bassett replied truthfully that (as the claim stood) there was not. He had no wish to alert the insurance company at this stage. Mrs. Abbott, Davis, all of them, might be totally innocent.

"You've been very kind," he said, as he prepared to leave.

Later Mrs. Fielding recollected where she had seen the name Jeffries before. A small item in a newspaper: *"A body, believed to be that of Mr. Justice J . . . who disappeared seventeen months ago, has been found in a remote cottage in Herefordshire . . ."*

Crafty thing, she said to herself, not without humour. It wasn't the Abbott claim you were interested in, it was Mr. Jeffries. You're engaged in—what do they call it?—tracing his last movements. She made a note, put all the paperwork she had sorted out for Bassett to one side for Mr. Dorridge's return, and smiled at the tulips.

As for Bassett, a thought crossed his mind: what if this Mrs. Abbott did not exist? But when he looked in the telephone directory there it was—one of three numbers under Abbott's Brook Farm: Mrs. A. Abbott.

FOURTEEN

Julie was occupied in the shop when Bassett paid his next visit to Davis's Garage. Davis's right-hand man, Stan, in white overalls and collar and tie, was standing on the forecourt in front of the office, talking to a smartly-suited gent carrying a briefcase, "salesman" stamped all over him. Bassett hovered. A glance through the office window had shown him that the office was empty. Stan raised a hand in greeting and presently was free.

"Needn't have hurried," Bassett said amiably.

"Glad to get away! Talk the legs off an iron pot, that one."

Stan was thin, thirty-five to forty, with a premature stoop and a vague air of melancholy. No misery, however, and when he smiled, first at the retreating back, secondly to inquire how he might assist Bassett, he became a good-looking man.

"Mr. Davis not in? Not to worry, I think you might be able to help me. Couple of queries." Bassett opened out the papers he had taken from an inside pocket. "About car hire. To a Mr. Jeffries."

"Jeffries?" Stan was slightly jolted, but there was no dismay that Bassett could see. "You are—?" The man twisted his neck to look at the papers. "Oh, insurance. Shall we go into the office?" He led the way.

"A Mr. Hugh Jeffries hired a car from you on several dates in '87 and '88," Bassett said when they were inside. "Nothing since. Except—a cover-note was made out for a hiring on December 17th, '88, and then cancelled. Question is: might that cancelled note have been made out for Mr. Jeffries? You see, the date corresponds to the date of Mr. Jeffries's disappearance eighteen months ago."

No hesitation. The blank look, the sudden loss of memory Bassett half-expected simply didn't materialize. "It is the same one, then?" the garage man said with some deference. "The Judge. The one they've found." The eyes became sad. "We did wonder at the time, when he went missing, saw it on TV. But they said he vanished from—was it Hereford?—so he wasn't likely to have been the Jeffries we knew."

"I don't follow—"

"We always imagined our Mr. Jeffries came from farther afield, by train. He used to collect the hire car at the railway station. Hereford? Why come here to hire a car when he could have hired one there?"

Good point. "The car was delivered, you say."

"To the station."

"And left there? Keys with the station staff?"

"No, he was usually waiting on the pavement outside. He'd take the car and run us back here."

"I get you. But he cancelled on that Saturday—"

"No, the car was delivered as usual. Nigel took it. The gaffer. Mr. Jeffries didn't turn up."

"Ah. He had to bring the car back. Were you here?"

"When he brought it back?" Stan shook his head. "I finished early. Knocked off that Saturday to take my young nephew to see Santa Claus."

Bassett regarded him thoughtfully. "You have an excellent memory, Mr.—er—"

"Harding. Stan Harding." He was one of those people who stand too close, crowd you, and listen extra attentively, eager to please. "The Judge's body in the news brought it all back to mind."

Bassett nodded, took a step backwards. "Understandable. Do you recall which car he was going to have?"

"Nigel's. The Carlton. I saw him take it, oh, just before ten o'clock. I packed up soon after. Only did a couple of hours. To show willing," he added, smiling.

"Did the gaffer often loan his own car out?"

"Didn't make a habit of it, no."

"Yet he did hire it out again, and it was written off. Very next day, if memory serves."

"Aye. Broke his heart. Mine too when I saw it."

"You helped to tow it in?"

A nod. "Winch job," the garage man said informatively. "Gaffer and I went out to it. Fine start to a Monday!"

Bassett grimaced in sympathy. "Oakleigh way, hit a tree, didn't it?" he said innocently.

Stan began a slow headshake. He was standing close again, his eyes on Bassett's as he spoke. "Nearer Lymock than Oakleigh. Went off road and down a bank."

He was in no measure menacing, but Bassett disliked being crowded so he was relieved when the telephone rang, drawing him away. "Do you mind?"

Bassett found himself listening to a one-sided conversation about tyres; watched Stan jot down instructions to himself; noted, no special reason, that the man wrote right-handed. Noted, while surveying the desk, the flowing handwriting on a sheet of paper bearing Nigel Davis's signature. The same hand had written the Jeffries booking. But not Mrs. Abbott's. That entry had been neat and painstaking. Not Stan's either. Examples of his handwriting now covered a sheet of jotting paper.

As the call ended Stan looked across at the window. "Here's Nigel now."

Nigel Davis appeared in the doorway.

"Nigel—our Mr. Jeffries. It seems he was the Judge after all."

Nigel Davis's face flickered on a frown. He was an athletic man with a mop of sandy hair, a slight swagger, and that certain something which, despite the overalls and collar and tie being no smarter than his right-hand man's, marked him as the more prosperous, the boss. He glanced questioningly at Bassett, cursorily at the copy documents Bassett seemed to present for his inspection, and at last found his voice. "The Judge? Bit of a shock."

A shout from outside had Stan running in response, Bassett calling a thank-you as he went. Then Bassett turned to Nigel Davis. "Matter of clarifying a few points, if you wouldn't mind, Mr. Davis. I gather you've already discussed the possibility of the Judge being the same man who hired cars from you, so you'll know what I'm talking about when I say the Saturday you delivered a car to the railway station. Date, December 17th. Client failed to show. Did you wait, in case the train was late?"

"Well, no. Glevebourne's not a busy station, it's easy to tell when a train's in. I hung on for ten minutes, then brought the car back. Wasn't keen to let it go in the first place. It was my own."

Bassett let that pass for the moment. "And when he was in the news, missing, a few days later, you didn't think to contact the police?"

One shoulder twitched. "Didn't seriously consider him to be the same man, to be honest."

"Occupation lawyer." Bassett referred to papers in his hand.

"But professions run in families," the other said. "We thought our Mr. Jeffries could be a relative. Which is why I didn't send a bill for time-wasting. Family worries—he didn't need me adding to them. Also, they found the Judge's BMW at the station. Why would anyone hire a car when he had one of his own?"

"Why indeed?"

"I cursed him though, on the quiet, afterwards. If he had collected the car it wouldn't have been standing doing nothing when Mrs. Abbott rang up on Sunday morning." The garage owner nodded towards the papers in Bassett's hand, the copy proposal form bearing Mrs. Abbott's name uppermost. "Bad for business to have to say no, and the lady's influential, puts a fair amount of sales trade my way. A week's hire—different tale, but a day . . . I was obliged to do her a favour. Same with the

Judge. His was a last-minute booking. I'd have fixed him up with a car of some sort even if my own hadn't been available . . . But all water under the bridge now."

"And lessons have been learnt," Bassett said. "It doesn't pay to loan out your own car." He smiled. "Did you lend your own car often?"

"Hardly ever before that weekend, never since. I keep a list of other hire firms instead. More than one way of being obliging. And I've plenty of new customers from the new estate anyway."

"Quite a boost to business, I imagine," Bassett said conversationally. "Still building, are they?"

"At the top end, yes."

"To recap then, Mr. Davis. Mr. Jeffries booked a hire car which he failed to collect. Booked by telephone?"

"The night before. Friday. Around four o'clock."

"He didn't collect, and you've heard nothing from his family, office et cetera since." Bassett gave him a direct look. "Wouldn't expect to, would you? Unless one of them knew he hired a car occasionally. Clearly none of them did or the police would have been here before now."

He folded his papers, made for the door. "Strange, his BMW at the railway station, his body found—what?—six miles, is it, to Oakleigh? Certainly adds to the mystery."

Nigel Davis nodded.

Bassett raised one eyebrow. "Mrs. Abbott had a lucky escape. Not hurt?"

"Few bruises, nothing serious."

"Lucky lady. Influential, you said." Address: Abbott's Brook Farm. "Farmers, are they? Poses the same question: why does someone in that position hire a car? Vehicles all over a farm, I'd have thought."

No reply to that: the telephone again. But for now Bassett was content. He had *some*thing. A tell-tale throb in the veins of Davis's neck. A tautness in the smile. A too-steady look . . . And that glibness when he was telling Bassett why he'd loaned his car out on the Sunday. Nigel Davis might almost have been trying to sell him something. And not a new car.

A lazy breeze brushed the forecourt. Stan Harding was manning the pumps. Bassett fetched his car, waited his turn. "May as well fill up, Mr. Harding, while I can." He noticed that the garage man used his left hand to trigger the gun, his right to screw on the petrol cap. "That's useful!" he observed. "You're ambidextrous."

The man laughed pleasantly. "Dicky middle finger. Look." His right hand, the middle finger, bent over to touch the palm. "Had it a few years. A nuisance at times. Can't grip anything in the palm of my hand."

"Ooh. Best check my petrol cap then, eh?"

"That'll be all right. I've trained the fingers I've got left. Strength's in them, the fingertips. See—?"

Another customer was arriving. Bassett took the hint. Julie emerged from the shop and assisted a dad pack bags and a string of toddlers into an estate car; saw Bassett and waved. He tooted his horn in reply, and caught sight of Nigel Davis staring out of the office window.

A few minutes later Nigel Davis descended the office steps . . . "Julie, that man you waved to. Who is he?"

"I think he's a Mr. Bassett," the girl said wisely. "Used to be a policeman. A detective chief superintendent."

FIFTEEN

Heather Davis had never been much of a housekeeper or cook, but she was trying. And discovering a talent for homemaking. There had been many moments during the past year when she had looked round her house and hugged herself, it was so nice, smelt so sweet. And shopping for food, freezing garden produce (compliments of Stan), cooking, baking, planning meals, were no longer tedious chores but adventures. She had often referred to her cooking, when she had done any, as "creative cookery." She had been expert at creating a mess. Now? Works of art. Well, nearly. All it took was *care,* advice reiterated by her mother throughout her life. Although not to Heather. For Heather was the pretty one, spoiled, petted, pampered, born to charm with her looks, kept on a pedestal, the doll . . . the farmworker's daughter nurtured to marry well.

Twelve years married; ten of them wasted.

She had said that to Nigel only the other night. He'd put a finger to her lips, told her not to say it again. All the same she wished . . . What did she wish? Nigel wished they could turn the clock back eighteen months; or else on, to when the Jeffries thing would be all over. She wished . . .

Yes! That was one thing she wished; that she could cure herself of grasshoppering; she had started out to plan what to cook for dinner tonight. Something quick and easy, Nigel had said just now. They had laughed, for that used to be her cry. Still, quick and easy it could be. Quick, easy, but *appetizing.*

Her pantry, fridge and freezer had never been better stocked, yet there was nothing in them that stimulated her taste buds. Which gave her a perfect excuse to go shopping. Food shopping. Her latest passion was shopping for food.

Upstairs to change. She hadn't altered that side of herself, hadn't discarded what some called vanity. Even for a shopping expedition she had to look good. She would wear her new cream suit and sandals.

Yes, and that was another job she must do, and soon, she commanded herself for the umpteenth time as she opened the door of a groaning, jam-packed wardrobe. She must have a clear-out: wigs to some amateur dramatic club, old evening dresses to an Oxfam shop; the state of her wardrobes was ridiculous . . . But the things were pretty, and they were hers. She knew she would hold on to them a while longer.

Dressed, made-up, her reflection in the mirror meeting with her approval, she checked her bag for cheque-book and pen and was halfway down the stairs when she heard the kitchen door open and close.

"Nigel? That you?" Her steps were carefree until she glimpsed his face. "What is it?" She guessed what it was. "Oh no." The colour drained from her cheeks.

"It's not what you think." Nigel Davis acquainted his wife with Bassett's visit. He spoke kindly, but when he had finished she looked shocked and affronted. He took hold of her hands, ice cold, shook them gently. "Stop worrying."

"Stop worrying!" It was little short of a hiss. "You said that when the body was found. Nothing to do with us, you said. Nothing to tie us in—"

"That still applies." He gave her hands a gentle pump.

She said, her beautiful eyes searching his, "What they were saying the other night—the gipsies did it. Did what, Nigel?"

"We've been over that. Pub talk—"

"But *did what?* Did *what?*"

"Did nothing," he said, pumping her hands. "Surmises. Because the gipsies had a go at the Judge in court. Stop worrying, *please.*" He gave her that half-frown, half-squint look she normally found so comical.

"On the radio, they said possibility of foul play—"

"Possibility."

"But *foul play*—" she entreated.

"Possibility of foul play. Foul play hasn't been ruled out. They're words, Heather, just words."

Were they? There was an ache round his heart too.

"Look, I'll have to go. Where are you off to? Shopping?" He looked her up and down appraisingly, kissed her on the tip of her nose, and drew away. "Good. Carry on as normal, as we agreed. You remember where the accident took place—"

"On the Lymock road. That stretch by Mad Willy's . . ." Her voice tapered off, then lunged. "That man. Nigel, who is he?"

"I've explained," he said patiently. "They're trying to establish Hugh Jeffries's last movements. Somehow they have discovered he hired cars from us occasionally. But they've seen the cancellation, they know he didn't turn up."

"So what makes you think they'd be interested in the accident?" Hysteria was moving in, and accusation. "You said you'd attended to it. You said it was foolproof—"

"It is." For God's sake! He also was desperate for comfort, couldn't she appreciate that? He didn't *know* who the man was. He had assumed, as Stan had apparently, that he was tracing Hugh's last movements. It was not till Julie said she thought he was an ex-policeman, and he'd sat down to think, that there began a slow understanding. Retired policeman turned insurance investigator?

He had cause to be wary of insurance investigators.

Nevertheless, he defied them to find anything wrong with that insurance claim. There was nothing wrong with it. *Nothing.* The claim had gone through without a hitch, for God's sake!

"It is foolproof, Heather. Believe me, love," Nigel Davis coaxed, but forgot to smile.

"Then why are you warning me?"

"Because they might ask questions of you. You're my wife, it was the family car that was smashed up."

"But why would they want to know about the *accident?*"

"Persistent little devil, aren't you?" At last he tried a smile. "The car was the car booked for Hugh. The only time my own car was loaned—or booked to be loaned—two days running. It's how their minds work. They may look for a link but they won't find one. Truly. Now, cheer up. I must go." He kissed the tip of her nose again. "A coward dies a thousand deaths, remember. If anyone does come—stick to the facts. Tell the truth."

He meant the truth as they had rehearsed it a long time ago.

Heather watched him cross to the door, wondered why the back of his neck looked suddenly so vulnerable and made her want to weep. "Nigel!" The command was soft, she was calmer now. "I'll be fine," she said, when he turned to look at her. "I will. Promise."

He grinned, gestured: you and me both, Babe. It had been their battle cry when they were teenagers.

She followed his progress out of the house and down the path. When he was out of sight she picked up the telephone.

Glevebourne Railway Station was half a mile from Davis's. A sleepy little station whose booking-clerk practised old-fashioned courtesy, made time to chat; and in retrospect recalled the BMW well.

"Two or three times we'd seen it in a corner; we half-suspected the owner of only using us as a car park, but we lost no sleep over it. Live and let live! It was quite safe, out of sight of the road . . . It was possible that he boarded a train, but the odd thing was none of us was able to give him a face . . . Oh yes, we knew it was a *him*, he was spotted, not actually getting out of the BMW but walking away from it, if you get my meaning. Walked straight out of the car park and down the road. It's all we ever did see of him, if I'm to speak the truth, his rear view . . . Picked up by another car? Well! Isn't that funny! It's possible, oh yes. Wait till I tell Maudie! She swore she saw him getting into a car once, pulled up at the side of the road. We thought she was talking through her hat. Out of one car into another? Don't be daft! we said . . . When? Oh, now you're asking. It wasn't the weekend we reported the BMW to the police, though, I can tell you that."

And so was of minimal assistance to Bassett.

"What colour was the car he got into?"

"Oh, I couldn't tell you. I don't think Maudie'd be able to tell you either. A car's a car to Maudie."

So Hugh Jeffries remained a shadowy figure, who came and went barely noticed. What an epitaph for a man.

SIXTEEN

"Mad Willy's Splash? There," milk-lady Jessie said, as she and Bassett pored over an Ordnance Survey map the next morning. It was on Jessie's round. It wasn't signposted, Mad Willy's was its local name; and don't ask her who Mad Willy was, he was long lost to antiquity. Not much of a brook there now, either. "There 'tis, there's the ford," Bassett said, as if Jessie knew what he was after, which of course she did not, the accident sketch-map being nowhere evident. His finger moved an inch, two inches, then stabbed. "There. It says Brook Farm."

"That's why you're lost!" Jessie exclaimed. "How old is this map? They call that Abbott's Brook Farm now. More up-market, as they say, than plain Brook. David Abbott's been there about seven years. Breeds rare cattle. What my dad would have termed a gentleman farmer. Doesn't soil his hands if he can avoid it."

Bassett pounced. "Got it! I know where I am now. There's a dip down one side of the road. Didn't a car go off the edge there about eighteen months ago?"

"That's right. One of those freak accidents."

"Freak?"

"The driver walked away. Lucky man. There's nothing much on that road, and nobody heard or saw a thing. He managed to get himself to the farm, so the story goes . . . If there ever was a man," Jessie said, lowering her voice. "Jill thinks Mrs. Abbott from the farm was the driver, but didn't like to admit it."

"Who is Jill?" Bassett inquired. "Someone who works there?"

Jessie nodded. "Tommy Martin's wife. She does some cooking for them."

Bassett was all set to probe, but a loud blast from a horn had Jessie running. Her Land-Rover was blocking the lane.

. . . .

Bassett hadn't neglected pup or chickens while he'd been galli-
vanting. It was his belief that it wasn't enough to feed and
house your animals, you had to spend time with them, love
them, talk to them, show them that they were wanted. So he had
spread out his investigations, interspersing them with trips
home, and keeping absences short. Sometimes he took pup
with him, other times he had left her at home to do what all
dogs do when bored: sleep. She slept a great deal, even normally. All the same, Bassett felt guilty. Today, Friday, was dry
and cooler than of late, ideal walking weather; and Abbott's
Brook Farm was within walking distance: three and a half miles
by road, but only two as the crow flies. Ergo . . .

"Sally!" It was her second cleaning day. "We're off now!" he
called to her upstairs. "Your eggs are on the table, and you
know where to put the key if I'm not back when you go."

"Leave it to me, Mr. B! Don't forget your knapsack!"

His canvas jaunting bag, into which he had packed a dish,
water and biscuits for pup, a small flask of coffee, bar of chocolate for himself.

Wild flowers and birdsong for the first half of the journey.
Bassett breathed in deeply. This was the life. Should have been
a country bobby like your grandpa, Bassett, old lad. Trouble
was, even in his youth village bobbies were a dying breed.

Peace continued when they joined the road. Only once did
Bassett have to scuttle like the rest of local wildlife out of the
path of an oncoming car.

Such was his mood that when he and pup reached the ford,
Mad Willy's Splash, and he saw no raised footwalk nor so much
as a stepping-stone, he was undaunted. How deep? Partway up
a duck! he joked. A shoes-and-socks-off job, anyhow.

Feet bare, trousers rolled up, not a soul in sight, he paddled
in and wriggled his feet on the bottom. Felt a strong sense of
déjà vu. Hadn't had tadpoles between his toes since he was
little! A jam-jar or an old tin can and he'd have had some of
them! "We've done this before, you and I," he told pup. "Fifty

years ago. Your name was Joe then and you were a mongrel. Ha! See! Did that before, as well. Always got me cap wet." This time it was his hat, floating back to where he had started from, pup giving watery chase. His third best, but he couldn't afford to lose it; he'd lost one already this week.

Mad Bassett's Splash from hereon, if perchance anyone *had* spotted him.

Abbott's Brook Farm was well-signposted. Big place. Miles of ranch-style white picket fencing. Wooded hills rising in the background. Far over, hairy cattle with massive horns; handsome animals whatever rare breed they were . . . Over the cattle grid and up the drive, which went on endlessly. The house was Georgian, an expensively refurbished farmhouse, brochures might say. Sweeping lawn, mature oaks, beds of roses in bud. At one side of the house a vast area of rhododendrons ablaze with colour . . . And eight or nine cars bearing late number plates parked in a semi-circle on a large expanse of gravel.

So many friends with cars, yet the lady had to hire one.

Pup's lead looped over the top of a fence post, hat plonked on top; pup to nap, the hat to dry. Knapsack on the ground, a hand through the hair, creases pinched back into trouser legs, and Bassett was no longer an old man out walking his dog. Now he was Bassett, ex-copper.

Thumb firmly on the bellpush.

"Coming!" The reply was a parade-ground roar, the man who opened the door, ebullient. "What kept you—!" At sight of Bassett the vigorous grin became an embarrassed smile. "Sorry, old man. Thought you were someone else."

Powerful build, sheen of good living, age around forty. Bleached eyebrows and hair, eyes blue and not unfriendly. This, the expensive shirt, the tailored corduroys, the gold watch below a rolled-up cuff, Bassett took in with a single glance: the gentleman farmer himself, surely.

"Mr. Abbott? Sorry to trouble you. I'd appreciate a word

with Mrs. Abbott. If I may? Nothing to worry her, tell her, but it
is rather important."

"I'll fetch her." The farmer moved, hesitated, his look evalu-
ating. "Give me some idea what it's about? Only there's a
Coffee Morning for some charity or other going on in there—"
One eyebrow shaped an inverted V. "And you know what
women are when they get together."

"Be assured I'm not selling anything," Bassett said affably.

The man winked. "Hang on."

Bassett was left standing on the steps. Ten seconds, and he
gave the door a gentle push; heard an interior door open on
girlish laughter and many female voices all talking at once: like
a distant gaggle of geese coming in to land. Heard the door
close, re-open, heard distinctly, "No, no. Nuisance . . . but
I'll see him." Dodged off the wide steps onto gravel. And had
his back to the door when Mrs. Abbott addressed him. "You
want to see me?"

He swivelled, smiled. "Oh, hello, yes. Admiring the rhododendrons, Mrs. Abbott. Magnificent display!"

"They are rather splendid, aren't they?" She was slim, had
shoulder-length light brown hair, wore pearls and a light blue
dress, and exuded charm and elegance. He had once thought
she might not exist, but here she was in the flesh. Beautiful
flesh. She smelt good, too.

Again he smiled, into a face flushed perhaps from hostessing.
"A query on car hire, Mrs. Abbott. Insurance, to be precise. On
a car you hired in December 1988."

He had wondered if her name could have been used without
her knowledge. But there was no denial, no puzzlement, only
lowered eyelids while she watched him unfold a bunch of papers, and a glimmer of interest when she looked up and met his
gaze.

"Computer's had hiccups, Mrs. Abbott. Would you mind
confirming a detail or two for our records?"

"Not at all," she said effusively.

"This is your signature?" On the copy proposal form.

She looked. "Oh yes."

"You had an accident."

"I did." A sort of mock-shame.

Or was she mocking him? He had the oddest feeling that she was. But she was doing it with great subtlety.

"The accident, Mrs. Abbott. Would you tell me about it? Briefly. It happened where?"

"Near the ford. To this day I don't know exactly what happened. One minute I was driving, the next I was sailing through the air, and the car—well, the car ended up at the bottom of the bank." A hand described an arc. Her nails were long and highly polished.

"What was the date, Mrs. Abbott?"

A moment's silence, then: "The date, as you very well know, was December 18th," she said, laughing, jollying him. "And the claim was settled months ago. So why this sudden urge to go over it all again?"

They stared at each other for some seconds. Bassett tried to read her mind, couldn't. "A careless remark," he said at last. "Overheard by someone—shall we say the wrong person? Who picked up a suggestion that the accident involved a man. That in fact at the time of the accident a man was driving."

"Oh, really!" She pouted: veiled disgust. Then threw her head back and laughed. "I'm sorry, Mr. Bassett, I didn't mean to be rude, but honestly! Shall I tell you how that came about? Some of our staff saw the car at the bottom of the bank while they were coming to work on the Monday morning. They ran down to see if anyone was trapped inside. For all they knew the accident had only just happened. Not unnaturally it caused some excitement. It got to me. Did I know anything about it? I spoke the truth. I told them the driver escaped unhurt.

"They took it for granted the driver was a man, and I have never to this day disabused them."

"Why ever not?" Bassett said.

"Call it pride," Alison Abbott said. "I didn't mind in the least people *not* finding out what a fool I'd been."

"Hardly a fool," Bassett said gallantly.

"A chump then," she said light-heartedly.

"A chump I'll go along with." Bassett made a face. "No broken bones?" he said solicitously.

She shook her head, smiled with her eyes. "Thank goodness."

"I'd better let you get back to your party," Bassett said, burying the papers deep into his pocket. His gaze seemed to drift lazily to the parked cars. "It's as well you didn't borrow one of your friends' cars. Why didn't you?" He tacked the question on casually.

"Most other times I would have been able to, but in an emergency—"

She didn't tell him what the emergency was, and he forbore to ask her. He knew she had improvised; he had no wish to push yet awhile. Especially to no purpose. To no purpose it would be. She was, he thought, one clever lady.

Bassett did not go all the way down the bank. Nothing would be gained from looking for paint flakes or fragments of Vauxhall Carlton here, no one had denied the *Sunday* accident. Quite the reverse. He and pup found a soft grassy spot partway down and there picnicked; albeit pup preferred Bassett's chocolate to her own food.

It crossed Bassett's mind that he also might be taking too much for granted: taking for granted that the car here had been the Vauxhall. It could have been some other.

But the longer he deliberated the more satisfied he became that this accident, Mrs. Abbott's, had been, for want of a better word—perfect. His main concern was the first accident, the Saturday accident, the one that might never have been.

The one they were concealing.

They. Who were *they?* Mrs. Abbott had addressed him by name. He hadn't introduced himself, and he was darned sure that coffee party was at the back of the house, so no one would have recognized him from a window. Yet Mrs. Abbott had known who he was. She had been tipped off.

"Know what I think, babydog? I think: conspiracy."

He heard tractor noise on the road above, heard the noise stop; paid little attention until he turned his head and saw, presumably, the tractor-driver moving towards him.

SEVENTEEN

"Just a-wondering who was here," the man said in friendly fashion. "Couldn't rightly see from the top." As he drew closer his smile broadened. "Oh-ho! Picnicking!"

Bassett got to his feet. "Are we trespassing?"

"No, you'm all right. Hello, little'un—" bending and putting his hands on pup, who loved it. "Seen someone was here, wondered who it was. I'm Darcy Jones, I works at the farm over there."

"Abbott's?"

"Ar. I gives them a few hours."

"You'm a lovely little'un, ent you?"

Bassett waited until the man looked up again, then: "My name's Bassett." He held up the coffee flask. "Cup to spare, Mr. Jones."

"Wouldn't mind at that!" the other said heartily. "Best call me Darcy though, same's everybody else." He sat on the grass next to Bassett. He had mutton-chop whiskers, rosy-apple cheeks, hairs in the dimple in his chin where a razor wouldn't reach, and eyes that had learnt to laugh at life. A real old countryman, more so than Tod Arkwright.

"Left school when I were thirteen!" he proclaimed. "During the war, that were. Found out they'd done away with beadles, none of them to come a-looking for me, so I never went back . . . Tom Mercer had the farm then. Went to work for Tom, stayed till he sold up. Sold me an' all, in a manner o'speaking.

Whoever got the farm got me along of it, that were the deal. Good gaffer, old Tom. Even though he sacked me reg'lar."

Bassett caught his eye. "Reg'lar as clockwork," Darcy said merrily. "And just as reg'lar I forgave him. This'un's only sacked me four times. I forgive him an' all. You 'ave to overlook their foibles." His laugh was infectious.

"Ar," Darcy said ruminatively, "him a-wedding young Alison mebbe made a difference to him keeping me on."

"Alison," Bassett said.

"Ar. He didn't have to, he could've bought me off. But good mates, little Alison and me, years ago. Carried her on my shoulders many a time, poor little beggar. And her sister."

Sister. Bassett started. *Sister.* "I don't believe I've met the sister," he said quietly.

"You don't come from these parts? No, mebbe not, then. Lives t'other side of Glevebourne. Wed the young fella from the garage . . . Ar, you've got it, Davis's. That's her name now: Heather Davis."

Mrs. Abbott was Nigel Davis's sister-in-law . . . Why the secrecy? Why Davis's "influential lady"? Why not "I could hardly say no to my wife's sister, could I?" Why not "My blooming sister-in-law bent it"?

"Alison was your little mate, did you say, Darcy?"

"Proud of her as I'd be of my own daughter," Darcy said. "Never had no nippers of my own . . . You live where? Or are you a-visiting like?"

"No, live here," Bassett told him. "Oakleigh, bought a cottage just before prices rocketed. Keep chickens. Had pigs till recently—"

They were on common ground. Soon they were two old countrymen deep in conversation, pup asleep on the grass between them. They talked pigs for a while, but gradually and adroitly Bassett drew the conversation back to Abbott's Brook Farm, and Alison Abbott and her sister. Darcy was happy to reminisce.

The two sisters had grown up in a cottage on Tom Mercer's

land; their mother had worked in the dairy; their father on the land. Good bloke, Frank Carrington, proud as a cock frog of his girls. Although he reckoned Alison, two years older than her sister, should have been a lad, the shortness and stockiness of her. Different as chalk from cheese, crab apples from peaches, the two girls were. Darcy had watched them grow up. Little Heather, born pretty, grew prettier and prettier, never seemed to go through an "okkard" stage. Queen o' the May more times than anybody could count, and of course, her mother being like his when it came to thinking above her station—an oblique reference to his name, Darcy?—pretty Heather was groomed for stardom, in a manner of speaking. Pretty clothes, pretty hair, taught to speak nicely, never allowed to get dirty. Big sister Alison was a carthorse by comparison. Thighs on Alison that could crush the ribs of a Suffolk punch. Playmates would think twice before they'd wrestle or play conkers with her. And she was plain as plain. An ugly little beggar, frankly, for most of her young life. Darcy used to feel downright sorry for the ugly duckling.

"Pretty'un seemed to have everything," he said. "My Alison nowt. Weren't true, mind; Frank and Maisie loved them both. But Alison—you couldn't dress her up pretty and she knowed it. Come Christmas or birthdays the pretty 'un'd want beads or ribbons. Alison'd choose books. And come party time, and the women fiddle-faddled over who was to wear what, Alison'd wander off and nine times out of ten hunt out her Uncle Darcy . . . Learnt her about horses, I did; and Nature. Wild flowers, trees . . . and when snow were on the ground how to pick out tracks. That be a fox made that 'un, I'd say. That be a rabbit . . . Followed me everywhere, the little'un did.

"Not as they was enemies, the two girls, never think that. No, the pretty'un was everybody's favourite, but it never turned her head. Stayed kind-hearted, her mum and dad wouldn't've had it no other way. Only thing I had against her—when she got older, like—was her pinching all the lads. Only nat'ral the pretty'un had all the lads after her, only nat'ral most lads'd prefer flirting to a fight; but anyone showed a feeling for Alison, Heather'd have him an' all.

"Mebbe it weren't her fault, mebbe she couldn't help herself no more'n they could; but I mind a time my Alison came a-crying to her Uncle Darcy. Heather didn't have to *go out* with him, she said; she didn't *have* to go out with him, she could've said no.

"Lads like that weren't worth a-bothering about, I told her. And mebbe it were Fate a-working, is what I've thought since.

"Odd how things turn out. Pretty'un had her day. Wed the pick o' the bunch when she were nineteen. Some of us reckoned her mother had hoped for even better, allus going on about Heather being a film star or swept off her feet by some heir to a title, head in the clouds half the time. But the pretty'un were allus getting herself into scrapes—ar, and trotting to Alison for Alison to sort 'em out for her. Before *and* after she were wed."

Not that Darcy had taken as gospel everything said about Heather. "You get a pretty'un—you'll allus get another as'll say she's no better than she ought to be. But I reckon Maisie and Frank figured it were time she settled down. And she did well for herself, there's no denying. Farm labourer's daughter wed to the Davis lad weren't bad, bit o' money there. But my Alison . . ."

Not to put too fine a point on it, his Alison had taken the lot of them by surprise.

"Allus was bright," Darcy praised. "Could've gone to university if she'd a-minded, but she didn't. Got herself a job with some fancy lawyers. Trotted off one day, down to Bristol, comes back a couple of years later, and I had a job recognizing her. My ugly duckling had turned into a swan. 'Tis me! Darcy, she says. Only she spoke better'n that. And I'm in love! she says, got me a wonderful man! You'll like him, she says. I won't have him 'less you do.

"Another two years before I met him, though. Comes back, wedding ring on her finger—Mrs. David Abbott."

There Darcy stopped for a breather, an expression of wonder on his face. His Alison! Done herself proud, his little mate.

"Sad thing, though," he said. "Frank and Maisie not being here to see it. Both gone. Went within a twelvemonth of each other."

A moment, then Bassett said feelingly, "Would that account for the delay in your meeting Alison's wonderful man, do you think?"

"D'you know, I never asked." Darcy shook his head slowly from side to side. "Odd you a-saying it, though, 'cause I allus had a feeling David Abbott weren't the man she'd been all excited about. The funerals—nobody came with her. No man. And she wouldn't stop, went straight back, hardly a word to Nigel and Heather. I think mebbe it didn't work out with the other fella. Ar, and if I was to put a mind to it I'd remember Heather went a-visiting Alison once or twice.

"But I ent a-saying no more 'cause it don't matter none. Not now. Come out on top has my Alison."

"And they are still friends," Bassett said, probing.

Oh yes. Sharpened their knives occasionally, but they were still friends.

And perhaps big sister Alison continued to help the pretty one when she got herself into scrapes, was Bassett's thought. He did not say it.

Instead he spoke about Stan Harding. "I think I do know the garage," he said. "Chap named Stan works there. Doesn't he come from round here?"

"Stan?" Darcy knew him well! "Straight bloke, Stan. Now he mooned over Heather from when they were kids, and led him a dog's life, she did. Fond of the lad, but it were never meant for him to hang his hat on her hatpeg and that were that. Her big brother now, the brother she never had. Watches out for her, like, when Nigel isn't around . . . Seems to have settled down, this last eighteen months or so. Started to grow up, mebbe. Though I don't reckon you should ever grow up altogether," he said with a chuckle. "Life's too short!"

"Stan's missus?" Later, Bassett probing again. "He wed Margaret Small. Good lass, more his type. But there you go again. Happy enough till they started building posh houses all round where they live; wanted her own, couldn't see why some should have and others not . . . Don't say as I blame her for that. Don't blame anybody for wanting to make something of themselves, but I never expected it of Margaret. Never expected her to go off and leave Stan . . . Mind, they do say as how he backed her all the way with her education, like."

"Gone to work in Bristol, I heard."

Seems to move about, Darcy said. "I think as how I heard she'd moved to Cheltenham a few weeks back . . ."

All good things have to end. Darcy said he'd best be moving too. "Or he'll be a-sacking me again! You wants to come to market, Tuesday. Sheep, o' course, mainly, this time o' year, but if you like pigs . . . You come. Anybody who's anybody in farming'll be there."

Mmm. A market might be the place to meet Mr. Abbott off his own patch. Alison too, perhaps. He'd like another talk to her. Was she still strong? Bassett wondered; still pack a good punch, could she?

He was saddened by his thoughts. He liked the lady. He'd liked Alison Abbott instinctively, on sight.

Bassett dropped in at the Tippers' on the way home. "That woman we were talking about, the one that made the telephone call. Can you recall if she made *two* calls?"

"No. No, only the one."

"And you didn't hear what she said."

"Had her back turned, spoke low," George said. "I think she knew the person she was speaking to. None of this spelling out of details. Know what I mean? Usually you have to give directions, all the details, tell them what you think is the cause of the breakdown, that kind of thing. Twice over, in my experience. There was none of that. She said what she had to say, and went out to wait for them."

"You went out, saw a car of some description with the woman's car. Twenty minutes went by, and you heard what you thought might be the breakdown truck. Anything else come to mind, George?"

George had been doing some cogitating: trying to link the woman's phone call with the Judge's disappearance; they had happened at around the same time, and it seemed strange for Mr. Bassett to be asking about a road accident, he had thought the other day . . .

"If it's any help," he said, "now that you mention it, the car I saw pull round the woman's car was nose pointed up, come in from the bottom end of the lane. Before the breakdown truck went past there was a car drove by, could have been that one, carrying on up."

"Stopped for a look, then carried on up the lane, is that what you mean?"

George Tipper nodded. "Only they must have stopped for more than a look, if you understand me, because there was a long gap between."

"But you've no idea what make of car."

"Lights, shapes, that's all you see in the dead of night . . ."

Bassett said he understood. "This was definitely the night of Saturday December 17th."

"It was." George Tipper could speak with confidence. He had been doing his own spot of checking up.

Must have stopped for more than a look. First a car, or it might have been a small van. Then—probably—the breakdown vehicle. Which of the two had come in response to the blonde woman's call? Who was in the car—a passer-by? Bassett pondered on this as he walked the remainder of the way home.

And on Alison Abbott who once had a job with "fancy lawyers." Guess that one of the lawyers was Hugh Jeffries before he made judge. Guess also that Jeffries was her "wonderful man."

Saturday: Judge Jeffries books a hire car but fails to collect—

so it is claimed. The car or its twin hits a tree in Long Lane; no accident reported, no witnesses. However, an unidentified woman telephones a service garage. Her car had *broken down,* she maintains.

Sunday: The car the Judge failed to collect is hired by—conceivably—a woman who knew him years ago. She has an accident *three miles away* from Long Lane. This accident is recorded, claim submitted and settled by the insurance company. All open and aboveboard.

And that was the trouble. The Sunday accident made a nonsense of the Saturday one.

EIGHTEEN

Two messages awaited Bassett when he got home. He read what Sally had written: "Jack the Poacher phoned, not urgent, says he'll phone again. 'Bob' says ring him as soon as possible."

He tried Jack's number; no reply. Dialled Glevebourne Police Station's number and was put through to Sergeant Andy Miller.

"Bob's got something for you, guvnor, but he's not here at the moment. If you tell me where you'll be in an hour from now I'll get him to contact you."

"I'll be at home, Andy. While you're on, could I beg a favour? I need information. Scuttlebutt stuff will do. Davis's Garage—the owner and his wife. And there's a man works there, Stan Harding. Also, while you're at it, if there's anything on the Abbotts of Abbott's Brook Farm. Is that too tall an order?"

"Give me a broom, I'll sweep up as I go along." Humour swelled the young sergeant's voice. "What do you want to know, guvnor?"

"Do you know any of them?"

"I know *of* all of them. Except for the Abbott bloke we all went to the same school. My sister Marion was in their class; I was a bit younger."

"You know *of* them. Give me a few f'r instances."

"Mrs. Davis and Mrs. Abbott are sisters, for starters. Heather Davis puts it around a bit. That's not gossip, that's fact. Husband Nigel plays three wise monkeys. A tough bloke in many respects, mean streak in him, good businessman, but soft as a brush with Heather . . . Stan. There have always been rumours about her and Stan, but I think you can take them with a pinch of salt. They might have before she married Davis, afterwards doubtful. Stan's too good a friend to Davis . . . Alison Abbott . . . she dropped out of the scene when Heather married. Left home to forge a career for herself. Came back as David Abbott's wife, so changed I for one didn't recognize her . . . David Abbott I don't know much about. Has money. Seems OK. Seems to have come by it honestly, I mean. Originates from Leamington Spa way, I believe."

"They were friends, your sister and Alison—?"

"Not really. Heather and Alison didn't have too many girlfriends. Heather was too fond of the boys to suit some of the girls' mothers, and Alison—she seemed to attract lame dogs. Nice kid, apparently. Used to sic the bullies off, that kind of thing. Sort of schoolgirl lone ranger. Marion always thought she'd go in for social work. Proves how wrong you can be."

"You say Davis knows his wife has affairs?"

"Knows. Accepts. She is what she is."

"How about Stan Harding's wife?" Bassett said. "Anything on her? Would your sister have known her too?"

"I can ask."

"She's missing," Bassett said. "By which I mean she is supposed to be working in Bristol or Cheltenham, but I sense an elusiveness. Point is, she seems to have done her nipping off about eighteen months ago. With me?"

"I'm with you. I'll get Marion to phone Stan, get her address."

"And when you have it—"

"Don't tell me. I'm to check it out."

"Good lad. One more thing, Andy—contents of Hugh Jeffries's pockets. Any receipts? Cheque-book?"

"Bob's beaten you to it." Bassett sensed the cheeky grin. "Beaten me to what?" he said.

"Cheque-stubs. We'd already got investigations going when our county friends took over, and Bob's still got info coming in. That's what he wants to talk to you about, I think, but I can give you some of it now. Hang on . . . Yes, here we are. The last three stubs, dated the day Jeffries went missing. One marked 'Bell's.' Whisky bill, we thought at first. Turned out to be a hotel near the Welsh border. Jeffries and a lady had a meal there on the evening of December 17th. The Saturday. The day he left Hereford. They'd been there about six times in a period of two years. Lady was a blonde. Well-dressed. Good-looker. Upper-crust."

"Memorable, why?"

"How do you mean?"

"Hotel. Hundreds of customers. Usually faceless. And this couple won't have been there for eighteen months. How come they remember so well?"

"Money, what else?" said Andy. "Always ordered the best, never quibbled over the bill, and he tipped generously."

"But they didn't know who he was?"

"That he was a judge? The missing Judge? Not a clue. As you say, faceless. Good customer, tipped well, blonde on his arm. These are what they remember."

"Same blonde each time?"

"Yep. They began to think she must be his wife. And they think they heard him call her Kerrie—"

Bassett interrupted. "Did you say *Kerrie?*"

"Mean something?" Andy sounded mildly excited.

"Nothing at all, Andy. Carry on."

"They heard him call her Kerrie, or something like it. But I'll come back to that, something there that Bob's working on. 'Nother item—the car. The manager at Bell's noticed Jeffries had a different car that night. Nothing special about it, just crossed the manager's mind that Jeffries had a new car. Couldn't tell us the make or the make of a previous car. What he was certain about was that he'd never seen Jeffries with a BMW. Means the car could've belonged to the lady. Bob's passed the info on, and our county friends are now looking for a woman named Kerrie or Carrie or Cassie, whom the Judge might've known."

Then it was back to the cheque-stubs. "One to Bell's. A second, for £20.00, went to staff at the Judges' House. The third was never presented, never went through the system. Could have been a gift for the lady."

"What's the amount?" Bassett asked.

"No amount. Slap-happy with his cheque-stubs, our Judge, hardly ever filled them in completely. Initials C. H. on this one, plus the date. Could make the lady's name Carrie, not Kerrie. Carrie . . . or Cassie? Cassandra . . ."

"Was that the first cheque he wrote?"

"No. First the £20.00, then C. H., then the hotel."

"Receipts—"

"None. Meticulous about filing his business receipts, and anything for the tax man, apparently. Others, receipts for pleasure, like the rest of us—seems to have chucked them. No sign of the hotel receipt."

"You said Bob was working on the Kerrie, Andy . . ."

"On the C. H. actually. The lady's initials? The list of Jeffries's colleagues includes a Henderson—and Bob knows of a Henderson, a solicitor, who moved to this neck of the woods about four years ago. He's checking it out. Checking the *wife* out."

"Right. You suggested the lady's name could be something that sounded like Kerrie, but could have been Carrie or Cassie—"

"Yes. And the H might not be an initial. It could stand for the gift he bought her. Hairdo. Honda. Hat. Holiday. Could even be an N not an H. Not a very neat writer, our Judge."

"Could also stand for something entirely different," Bassett said. "Car hire, for instance. But if we could stay with the woman's name for a moment, Andy. The hotel staff *thought* they heard Jeffries call the lady Kerrie. Implies that they *overheard*—so what he called her might have been a private name, a pet name. What was Alison Abbott before she married—was it Carrington?"

Good bloke, Frank Carrington, Darcy Jones had said.

"Carrington," Andy repeated. "D'you know, I think it was."

"And I have it on good authority that when Alison went off to forge herself a career she ended up working for lawyers. Are you with me?"

"I'm way ahead of you, guvnor."

"Right. A word in your ear. You and Bob are off the murder case—but what I'm working on is insurance fraud. Car insurance. No skin off my nose who solves the murder. But if an insurance fraud investigation leads by chance—"

Andy cut Bassett short. "Nuff sed. And guvnor? I've a few days owing to me. And what I do in my own time is my business."

"I might take you up on that," Bassett said. "Check Margaret Harding for me. We'll see what Bob has to say about Henderson. Then we'll get together on it. In the meantime there's much I haven't figured out, so I'll put me thinking cap on."

"I'll get on to Marion straightaway, and—oh, yes! that reminds me—" Accusation flowed down the line.

"What?"

"When are you coming in to pick up your hat?"

Bassett hung up on Andy's laugh.

Bassett pottered, mulling over what Andy had told him. The three cheques: written by Hugh Jeffries on—it could be assumed—the last day of his life. First, a Christmas box for people who had looked after him in Hereford—on to Glevebourne to collect and pay for a hire car—on in the hire car to Bell's Hotel. The sequence made sense.

Sense could be made, also, of the hire-car cheque not finding its way through the system.

A blonde accompanying Jeffries to the hotel fitted in with a blonde who later *that same night* made a telephone call from the Tippers'.

Question: who was the blonde?

She had either to be Mrs. Davis or Mrs. Abbott. He was convinced of it. True, neither was a blonde now—but Mary had worn wigs for special occasions, why shouldn't they? And anyhow, fortunes were spent on hair colourants.

Alison had once worked for lawyers. He had already guessed that Jeffries was one of them, that he had perhaps been her lover. Now, bearing in mind Darcy's hints about Heather and the visits to Alison while she worked away, Bassett reasoned that on one of these visits Heather met Hugh Jeffries. She was accustomed to pinch her sister's boyfriends. Suppose she had done so again. That would tie in with what Wanda Jeffries said about her brother being serious about a girl until something— or someone—fouled it up . . . Heather had an affair with Jeffries, Alison quit and married someone else—David Abbott.

Heather? Or Alison? Which sister had met Jeffries again, years later, and had taken up where they left off?

On feasibility alone Bassett had Alison as the lady. Hugh Jeffries had been serious about someone, sufficiently serious for his sister to have noted and remembered. He subsequently never married. Why not? Because he had been hurt, or had hurt himself. A man doesn't moon the rest of his life over an infatuation. He *might* over the woman he truly wanted but had foolishly lost . . . And to meet her a second time . . .

It had to be Alison. She and Hugh would have had similar interests, a similar level of intelligence. If their love for each other hadn't died . . .

Bassett sighed. A tired sigh. He had remembered a little more of his conversation with Darcy Jones. Heather seemed to be settling down at last. Since when? Bassett asked himself.

Since something happened to shock sense into her? *Eighteen months ago?*

He shelved the question, rang up his own garage.

"Phil, suppose you had cars for hire and your sister-in-law wanted loan of one, what would you do?"

"Lend her one, if I had one available."

"What about insurance?"

"Tell her to contact her insurance brokers and have her own insurance transferred for the duration."

"If she was only insured third party—?"

"I'd suggest separate insurance cover. I'd want a car of mine covered fully comprehensive. On the other hand—I'd most likely tell her to be extra careful."

"What if she bumped it?"

"I'm in the right place to do my own repairs."

"What if she wrote it off?"

"I'd throttle her."

"Seriously."

"Seriously, I wouldn't be very happy. I'd be in trouble. Why? Got a problem? Or is this just a general inquiry?"

"General inquiry, Phil." Bassett chuckled. "Sorry if I've spoilt your day."

"Shan't be lending my car to anyone in a hurry, that's for sure!"

"Transfer own insurance." Bassett filed this away for future reference. Not that Phil's answer had been of great assistance. How do you contact brokers on a *Sunday?*

Nor did Bassett expect miracles from his next call, but it was a call he had to make. There was a remote possibility that the Vauxhall Carlton, some of it, was standing in a vehicle graveyard somewhere. A remote possibility that he might yet find something to prove that the Judge had been in that particular car. A chance in a million, but stranger things had been known.

"Smith's Auto-Salvage? Good day to you! I require bits for a Vauxhall Carlton. A friend recommended you."

"Good for him!" a youthful eager voice said at the other end of the line. "What are you looking for, sir?"

"What do you do, salvage re-usable parts?"

"Top quality only! Wheels, engines, gear-boxes, alternators, radiators, lamps—you name it. Not certain about Carlton bits, don't see too many Carltons, but some Vauxhall bits are interchangeable. If you tell me what you want I'll go and check—"

"Matter of fact," Bassett said, "a friend told me you had a Carlton in recently. I thought I might come and pick out a few emergency spares."

"No, not us." The voice was low, apologetic. "Long time since we had a Carlton in." It rose a notch. "You wanted to come and see the car as a whole and buy spares off it, is that what you mean? People can do that but they have to be quick. We strip them down and send the bodies for re-cycling as fast as we can these days. Take up too much space."

"Where do the bodies go when they leave you?"

"Holt's. I don't think you'll have any better luck there, if it's a Carlton from here you're thinking about. Oxo-cubed and off within a month usually. Where are you calling from? We've a shop here, you could always come and have a look round, might find what you want," the voice said helpfully.

Might. But Bassett doubted it now. He thanked the youth for his assistance and took himself belatedly off for a bath. He needed one after the walk.

Afterwards, a lazy hour in the garden. It was that time of day, mid-afternoon, when little stirred. Pup slept, worn out after her morning exercise; the hens had ceased pecking for a while, and with bellies full dozed on the backs of the garden chairs, occasionally dropping their half-crowns where they shouldn't. For Bassett it was a peaceful hour with a pipe to gather his thoughts.

He knew now that he had no proof—never would be able to obtain proof—that the Vauxhall Carlton hit a tree on the precise day he believed it had: *the day before Alison Abbott hired it.* No proof that the car that hit the tree was the *very same car* the Judge had been booked to have. It *could* have been the Carlton's twin, owned by a perfect stranger. A good lawyer would make much of the possibility of coincidence, ridiculous though it might appear to be.

And yet Bassett knew also that he had the answers, the ones that counted; the ones that would give him his murderer.

"Like a pot of poor man's stew," he muttered once to himself. "You know the meat's in there, you can smell it, you just can't catch it in the ladle."

He took a cottage pie out of the freezer, put it in the oven, set the timer for an hour . . . and had finished eating when Andy Miller came back on the telephone.

"Margaret Harding is in Cheltenham, guvnor. Moved there about two months ago from Bristol. Marion couldn't have much of a chat with her, she was in the office—"

"But she's alive and well, which is all I wanted to know, Andy. Thank you. I did think we might have another body to look for. Is Bob back yet?"

"He's here, breathing down my neck."

Bob Greenaway took over the telephone. "Henderson was a non-starter, Harry. No go."

"Not to worry, Bob, I have a few ideas of my own. Had time to check the list for Carrington?"

He had. Alison Carrington had not worked for Hugh Jeffries's firm.

Granted, the list only went back four years, but the secretary there, a Miss Hartland, had been with the firm forever.

NINETEEN

Jack the Poacher had news of information that might help launch an appeal for Aaron and Isaac Smith.

Jack hadn't bothered to ring up again. He arrived in person. He had been to see Aaron in prison, and also some of Rosie-from-Hereford's neighbours. Two neighbours stood out: nice Barbara Robinson, and Alice Cooke, otherwise known as Skin and Grief.

"It was Alice who laid the poison down for Aaron and Ike," Jack told Bassett. "She seldom had a good word for anybody—Rosie was one of the few who got on with her—but she had no time whatsoever for the Smith lads.

"Apparently Rosie was a great giver. As soon as she was back on her feet after her first stroke she started giving her possessions away, much to Barbara's consternation. You'll have an empty house, Rosie! . . . Oh, what does that matter, Barbara! I want to see the expressions on people's faces; can't do that when I'm dead, can I?

"Aaron's interpretation of events on the night of the so-called burglary had Alice finding Rosie, calling the police, the police asking questions, and Alice supplying the answers she thought they wanted to hear. Aaron and Ike had seen empty shelves—the police had seen what to them would have looked like a *ransacked house*. They would have asked the obvious question: any strangers, unusual characters, in the area recently?—and Alice might have replied quite innocently, yes, gipsies. Any idea of what may be missing?—yes, a basket of porcelain . . . And the police took it from there."

"That presupposes Alice knew of the porcelain," Bassett said.

"Barbara said she did. According to Barbara, there was nothing innocent about Alice's replies. She thinks Skin and Grief was probably feeling vindictive—because she'd been hoping to have the porcelain herself. It was true, Rosie had stored the basket in her junk room. Barbara herself hadn't known of its existence until after Rosie's stroke. But she and Alice knew that Rosie had willed the house to her son, contents to neighbours and friends on a sort of take-your-pick principle. And while Rosie was laid up Alice went ferreting . . . She thought I was a goner, Rosie told Barbara. Found the porcelain, thought, Oh!

I'll have that!—added a few more items, and put them on one side, her name on them, so to speak.

"Rosie recovered. Showed Barbara Alice's cache, had a chuckle over it. Poor Alice. She could have the extra items, but not the porcelain.

"Rosie did intend Aaron and Ike to have it, she virtually told Barbara so. Aaron and Ike had done her a great favour with the clock, probably the greatest favour of her life; she was always on about them. But that wasn't the only reason she wanted to give it to them . . . What a pity it is, Barbara, Rosie said, to pack things out of sight because you think they might be broken or stolen or something. These pieces haven't seen daylight for decades. I'm going to give them to people who'll *enjoy* them, enjoy them for what they are . . . As Barbara said—gipsies adore china and porcelain. Rosie was aware of the fact. Unfortunately, in court, Barbara had to admit that Rosie hadn't actually named Aaron and Ike as the prospective recipients.

"Same with the wrappings. Alice testified that she had only seen *old* wrappers on the porcelain. No doubt true. Barbara likewise. But when Rosie showed her the porcelain the basket was half-unpacked. She's convinced that Rosie was unpacking the stuff preparatory to washing it and wrapping it in clean paper. In other words it was Rosie herself who re-wrapped it, not the lads. Again, however, she didn't *see* Rosie re-wrapping it, so—no go.

"Anyhow," Jack said, "remember my saying there was a question of a letter Rosie wrote to her son? Barbara vaguely recalls Rosie saying something about a letter to Arnold to explain about the porcelain. It was said at one of those times when you're half-listening, half-not, and Barbara was never absolutely certain Rosie said it. She thought she did, but it might have been a kind of wishful thinking on her part. She didn't mention it at the time of the arrests, Barbara said, because in the urgency of the moment it simply didn't occur to her. When eventually she did twig what was going on, nobody seemed interested. If there had been a letter, the son would have produced it—that seemed to be the general response. She kept hoping the son would turn up so that she could have a word with him. But everything was handled by solicitors.

"The son instructed them to sell the house. Barbara was street executor, distributed Rosie's remaining belongings. And that was it. No mention in the will about the porcelain, apparently.

"Now I'll get to the point," Jack said with a grin. "I've tracked down the son. He's a Bush Brother. A priest. On an aborigine reserve in South Australia. Pal of mine in Adelaide is working on it now. He's spoken to the man, tells me he remembers the letter but not Rosie's wording about the porcelain. He's currently on walkabout, won't be able to check until he gets back to base, but—there it is, Harry, a ray of hope."

"And I have another," Bassett said. "What do you know about the Abbotts?"

"Abbott's Brook bloke? I've met him, don't know him very well."

"I won't offend you then if I say the Abbotts are on my suspect list."

Bassett's first stop the following morning was at Glevebourne Police Station. He made his request to Sergeant Miller. "Andy —Miss Hartland's address—"

"Great minds . . . She retired a year ago. Tewkesbury. That's where she lives now." He handed Bassett a slip of paper. "Telephone number's down there, too."

"How goes it?" Bob Greenaway asked.

Bassett looked from him to Andy and back again. "Mind if I sit down, rest my weary eyes?" The other two hunched shoulders at each other. Andy drew Bassett a chair.

And so Bassett re-told, much condensed, eyes closed, off the record, what he had recounted to Jack the evening before.

"I believe Mrs. Abbott was out with Hugh Jeffries on that night eighteen months ago. I believe she met him in the course of her work—probably met Abbott similarly. I believe she might have married Jeffries—didn't—ended up with Abbott instead, but still hankered after Jeffries, and took up with him again.

"The car everyone is looking for no longer exists. It belonged to Nigel Davis. They took Long Lane too fast, hit a tree. Trouble is, we'll never be able to make out a case because that same car, Davis says, was hired by Mrs. Abbott the following day. She wrote it off by rolling it down a bank not far from where she lives—and we'll never be able to prove that she didn't. On paper it was a genuine accident. The car was seen at that particular spot, an accident claim was put in, everything done according to the book: claim settled, wreck to salvage firm. Car extinct.

"Between the time Jeffries bumped the car in Long Lane and the time Mrs. Abbott is said to have taken it out, someone finished the poor man off by thumping him on the head with a rock. In fact, I believe that was why Mrs. A hired the car the next day—to cover up the murder.

"I'm not saying Mrs. Abbott did it. But one of them did . . . Five suspects. Mrs. Abbott. Husband David. Mrs. Davis. Nigel Davis. And Davis's right-hand man and friend of both Davises, Stan Harding.

"Why the Davises and Stan Harding? Because, having told you what I think happened, I confess I may be wrong. It could have been Heather Davis who was out with Hugh Jeffries.

"It was one of the two, I'm sure. Mrs. Abbott or Mrs. Davis. I intend to find out which. How? I'm going to keep at 'em, keep popping up to ask a question; break them down. There's usually a weak link somewhere, I aim to find it."

Finished speaking, Bassett stood up. "Talking of popping up," he said slowly to Andy's intent gaze, "if you are passing Davis's Garage—? Needn't do or say anything. Just show yourself now and then." He looked at his watch. "I'm off there myself now. See you."

•   •   •   •

There had been one in virtually every garage workshop Bassett
had entered: a grubby little urchin with a pudding-basin hair-
cut, wearing overalls several sizes too big, crutch down at the
knees, exposed flesh covered in grease and grime; often more
willing than useful, and usually unsackable by any but the
stone-hearted because of puppy-dog eyes and a sunny disposi-
tion. This one's name was Fred, diminutive for Freda; she was a
girl. "Outside and underneath only," he learnt during the
course of their conversation: she was too grubby to work inside
a car, even with a dust sheet.

Happy little soul, though, and as luck would have it she was
working on a Vauxhall, doing an oil change, so it was a simple
matter to lead the conversation to Vauxhall Carltons, and spe-
cifically the gaffer's. Oh yes, Fred was here when they brought it
in as a wreck. Cut up real bad, was Nigel. Looked bad for a
week, right up to when they knocked off for the Christmas
break.

"Some woman, wasn't it?"

"So they said. Took the mickey out of me something rotten,
that lot"—the other mechanics—"just because I'd been lectur-
ing them on women being safer drivers than men." She directed a scowl, but Bassett wasn't fooled, it was all pretence. He
laughed, sharing in the joke. "Do you know who she was?" he
said, continuing the spirit of the thing.

"No, never saw her."

"Weren't you curious?"

"Her name probably wouldn't have meant anything to me
anyway. I think we did ask, casual like. Some woman who won't
get a car from me again, was all Nigel said."

Some woman. A name, Alison Abbott, on official forms.
Anonymous, "some woman" to garage staff, insurance assessor, anyone who might know the lady.

Nigel Davis wasn't so easy to pin to one spot. Saturday mornings were busy. But even he had to stand still sometime. That
was when Bassett moved in, office empty, Davis snatching a
stand-up coffee break. "Ah, Mr. Davis. Sorry to bother you

again. Small query came up on a cheque Mr. Jeffries made out on the day he booked a hire car from you."

"Cheque?"

"Made out for car hire, according to the stub."

Davis shrugged, drank coffee, repeated the shrug. "It never went through my books."

Bassett nodded. "That's what we find odd. The cheque seems not to have gone through anyone's books. Wasn't in the cheque-book or loose in his pocket."

"So? He probably tore the thing up!"

"What we can't understand is why Mr. Jeffries should have written a cheque in advance—"

"Why shouldn't he?" Davis said impatiently. "If I gave him a figure when he rang up—"

Bassett appeared to pounce. *"Did* you?"

Davis's eyes flashed. "I must have done, mustn't I, if he wrote a cheque. Look—" He started fussing; break ended, he wanted to be off, work to be done. "I've told you all I know. He was a customer. He let me down. OK? That's it. Finish. Now if you'll excuse me—"

"There is one other item, Mr. Davis. I regret having to mention it, albeit I often learn more from what people *don't* tell me than from what they do." Bassett might almost have been apologizing. "Why didn't you tell me Mrs. Abbott is your sister-in-law?"

In Bassett's opinion Davis's answer should have been "What the hell has that got to do with Jeffries and a cheque?"—or else nothing at all. Instead, the man paused for thought and answered blithely, "I daresay it never entered my head." And the awkwardness with which he said it spoke volumes.

What would the reaction have been, Bassett wondered, if he had asked the man how he got along with his sister-in-law?

Leaving the office, he turned in the direction of the Davis house. Time he spoke to Heather Davis.

•   •   •   •

She was outside, rubber gloves, duster in hand, polishing glass panels on either side of the front door. The strikingly pretty woman he had seen in the garden the other day. Darcy's Queen of the May. Whose eyes danced, until he told her his name.

He deflected any possible rebuff by giving her one of his best smiles, and saying, "I fear I've come at an inconvenient time, Mrs. Davis. But if you could spare me five minutes . . ."

A hand fluttered. Not quite a negative gesture.

"I'm still puzzling out the Jeffries case."

Perhaps it was the "puzzling," perhaps it was the hangdog expression, perhaps it was her own common sense, but Heather Davis's face took on a smile. "Oh," she said, and stopped her dusting. "I'm not all that busy," she said candidly. "Showing willing, really."

Of course. Bassett couldn't imagine her tackling heavy housework; she hadn't the staying power, surely. Too dainty. Too fragile. A little girl playing house was the impression he gained. Although he recognized that he might be deceiving himself: she might be tougher than she looked.

"Are you having any luck?" she said.

"I think so. Getting there slowly but, as they say, surely." Their eyes locked briefly; hers sprouted a frown.

As if to explain it, Mrs. Davis said in a rush, "I'm an awful worrier, Mr. Bassett. I've been worried ever since Nigel told me it was the Judge who hired cars from us. We didn't tell the police. If only we had it might have made a difference."

"A difference to what?" Bassett said kindly.

"People's memories would have been sharper, someone could have remembered seeing him . . ." She faltered. "I mean . . ." Bassett watched her thoughts slide into the distance and back. "I mean . . ."

He rescued her. "You mean that although the Judge failed to collect the hire car, he must have come to this part of the world. And if you had spoken up at the time someone somewhere might have recollected seeing him, whereas now it's a little late in the day."

"Yes. That's what I mean." Her face softened with gratitude. "I'm not very good at expressing myself."

Breeze lifted a wisp of hair on her temple, a small movement caused her hemline to sway fractionally. Bassett questioned, not for the first time in his life, why some women thought they had to doll themselves up to the nines to look fetching. Her cheeks pink, her clothes summer-fresh rather than fashionable, her hair untidy, Heather Davis could not have looked more attractive.

He smiled. "You're doing fine."

She dimpled.

"What I can't understand," Bassett said slowly, "is why your husband didn't tell anyone it was your sister who hired the Carlton."

"My sister . . . ?" she said in a sing-song, little-girl manner.

"The following day," Bassett said. "Sunday."

"Oh. Oh yes!" Silly me.

Bassett inclined his head, knuckled the side of his nose. "I'm a funny cuss, I know, but if my car had gone for a burton I'd have had to say it the once. Wouldn't have been able to resist it."

"Say what?" Mystified.

"Blooming sister-in-law bent it!"

"Oh!" She laughed.

"And it's most people's favourite pastime—having a go at other people's driving," Bassett said cheerfully.

"Oh, but you don't know Alison. She's very reticent, tells nobody her business, never has. You can tell Alison anything, she won't repeat it . . . So it wouldn't have been fair of us to spread the story behind her back. If she'd wanted people to know she would have told them herself . . . Nigel did his share of complaining, though, I can tell you. Most of it to me," she added with a wry grin.

Bassett smiled in sympathy. She really was lovely, he thought. He jotted down his telephone number on a page of his notebook, tore the page out and gave it to her. "If you do think of anything, Mrs. Davis—"

"Oh! Is that all?" she said, astonished. "Well, that was pain-less, wasn't it?" She laughed; said with a definite fervour, "I feel awful, not inviting you in. You could have had a cup of coffee, or a sherry . . ."

Bassett motioned. "Another time, perhaps." He hated to dim the light in her eyes, but needs must. He tapped the note-book as he closed it. "I see that Mrs. Abbott was a secretary to a firm of lawyers before she married."

The light did not dim, it shone more brightly. "That was a long time ago, Mr. Bassett."

She watched him go, went indoors, tore off the gloves and threw them across the room. Damn Alison!

Bassett sat in his car and pondered. Could it have been Heather Davis who donned the mantle of sophistication when out with the Judge? Could she do it? Could she walk, talk, conduct herself like a lady?

Yes. Yes, she could.

But he still favoured Alison for the part. She could have done it better. Alison *was* a lady.

At home, he rang up Miss Hartland, made an appointment to meet her in Tewkesbury at one o'clock, and spent the rest of the morning having a romp with pup.

TWENTY

They met for lunch at the Black Bear, a timber-framed old coaching inn whose garden stretches down to the banks of the River Severn. Miss Hartland's suggestion. "I'd love to meet you," she said when Bassett rang her up. "I would invite you to tea, but unfortunately I have decorators in. There's the Black Bear . . . Although this continuing good weather will have brought out a rush of weekenders in their boats and barges; the place will be busy . . ."

"The more the merrier!" had been Bassett's reply. He realized that might have been the idea. An elderly lady if she lived alone would do better *not* to invite a strange man into her home.

There was nothing *elderly* about Miss Hartland. She was neat and trim, might have been any age from forty on, and was, Bassett was to discover, great fun. Her smile was spontaneous and natural, and not only reached her eyes but remained there.

"You said you were retired," she said, introductions over, "but I can see you're like me—treating retirement as a beginning. Did you look forward to it in the end?"

"Could hardly wait."

"Same here. All I'd ever had was my job and for many years dear but clinging parents. A lifetime spent doing what other people wanted me to do. Oh!"—she veritably hugged herself with her words—"freedom to please myself is very sweet!"

"An end to duty!"

"An end to duty," she said gaily, "as you say."

They had taken to each other immediately, and over their first drinks Bassett found himself telling her about Mary and the plans that had gone awry. By the time their man-size steaks and salad had been eaten they might have been old friends, well-met.

"Did you have the career you really wanted?" she asked. "So many people don't, you know."

"Career." Bassett pursed his lips comically. "Ha! What I'd really have liked to be was a tramp."

"A man after my own heart!" she exclaimed. "You do mean a tramp of the world—"

"Most certainly. No fun tramping in English winters. What a way to start the day, eh? Bacon and coffee cooked on a camp fire . . . Never tastes quite the same when you cook it indoors."

"Mmm." She sniffed the breeze. "It's never too late, is it?" she said wickedly. "Could still be done."

Bassett chortled. "Imagine it! Think of the ever-growing population of pensioners—and hoards of us all hiking it with our walking frames."

"Covered in pots and pans—"

"Ha! Exactly. That was one of the things that put me off—having to carry great loads of gear with me."

They both laughed. Coffee was served. "You want to know about Hugh," she said soberly. "May I ask you something? I was very fond of Hugh. How did he die?"

Bassett couldn't lie to her. "We believe he was murdered. But until the coroner's verdict—"

"I understand. What would you like to know?"

"He never married."

"No."

"His sister, Wanda, says he was serious about a girl nine, ten years ago. Would she have been a girl named Alison Carrington?"

"Oh dear. Is Alison involved?" Her face fell.

Bassett apologized. "I'm sorry. I should have made myself clear. We require information in order to eliminate as well as to apprehend. Miss Carrington's name came up—"

"Oh, I see. Well, the answer's yes. Hugh was very taken with her. Smitten is the word, I think. She was different from his previous girlfriends. Well-mannered. Well-groomed. Patient: no tantrums from Alison when he was late leaving the office. A charming girl."

"She didn't work with you?"

"Our firm? No. She was with Bellamy's. Hugh met her there. But I did get to know her fairly well. She'd come in for a chat after work, while she was waiting for Hugh. She too was smitten, or perhaps the word I should use for Alison is spellbound. She was a trifle unworldly in the beginning. I did wonder if it wasn't the glamour of Hugh's profession which attracted her to him—glamour in the sense that a lawyer was so removed from her own background. I can't believe that a man like Hugh would be keen on *me*, she said once. She reminded me of myself when I was a little girl and woke up one Christmas morning to find Santa had left me the most beautiful doll ever. I simply refused to believe the doll would not be taken away. I kept asking my parents: are you *sure* it's mine, are you positive it's mine? Santa hasn't made a mistake? That was Alison, too. Her eyes sparkled, she *looked* like a girl in love." She sighed. "And then—it ended."

"Do you know why?"

"No. Hugh never uttered a word on the subject. He went into a shell. Came out of it twice as ambitious as he had ever been . . . And some weeks later I heard that Alison had married David Abbott."

"Did Hugh ever call Alison Carrie?"

"Carrie? Yes. Yes, he did. He didn't like the name Alison for some reason."

"Did you meet Alison's sister, Heather?"

This time a headshake. "I never *met* her. Alison spoke about her, said she was a pretty girl. She seemed to be very fond of her."

"Miss Hartland, may I ask if you have any idea of your own about Hugh and Alison . . . ?"

"About why they split up?"

"Yes. Did you never hear anything—a word here, a nod there—?"

"There was a general feeling among Hugh's friends, myself included, that David Abbott's money . . . I heard on the grapevine that she had been seen with David Abbott while she was still walking out with Hugh. If she could hook Hugh, why not try for bigger fish? But we were all biased towards Hugh." She smiled, a trifle sadly. Bassett waited. But all she said afterwards was, "We may have misjudged Alison."

With which Bassett had to be content.

•   •   •   •

It rained overnight. More rain was forecast for later. But for an hour or two the sun shone. Bassett put himself a slow roast in the oven, a lead on pup, his pac-a-mac in his pocket, and set off to find Tommy Martin and wife Jill.

The Martins lived in a council house, one of a row of six, halfway between Oakleigh and Lymock.

Tommy wasn't at home. Jill was. As good-natured as they come. "You're the honorary village bobby! Heard of you. What's he been up to?" she joked. She was busy with baking tins. "Don't mind if I carry on, do you? Only the oven works overtime on a Sunday and I'm a bit behind."

Bassett sat on a stool just inside the kitchen door, and pup, at Jill's invitation, flopped underneath the table. Play her cards right, pup might win herself a titbit.

"Is it about the Judge?" Jill said, rolling out a lump of pastry. "Jessie said you wanted to know if Tommy had seen anything. Nothing, I'm afraid. Like Jessie, he never really *looked*. But he never noticed anything out of the ordinary. Nothing that he can remember."

She appeared to take for granted that Bassett was resting after his walk, and told him to help himself to a cold beer out of the fridge, she was that kind of lady. Bassett declined. Stayed. Said presently, "You work for the Abbotts, don't you?"

"Do some cooking. Part-time, so it's a good little job for me. And Mrs. Abbott pays well."

"Settle an argument for me. That car that went off the road near the ford. Who was driving? Was it a man or Mrs. Abbott herself?"

"Mrs. Abbott," Jill mouthed. Aloud, just: "She let everybody think it was some man or other . . . but it was her," mouthing once more, as if she were gossiping in the Abbott's kitchen and walls had ears. "Thea told me."

Thea was Mrs. Abbott's housekeeper.

"What happened," Jill went on, spooning jam into pastry cases, "was that Mrs. Abbott's car broke down the night before. At least, she didn't say, but she'd gone out in her own car at dinner-time, came home in her sister's that night. Doesn't take brains to work out that hers had packed in and she had borrowed her sister's while her own was being repaired."

"Her sister being married to a garage owner."

"That's right. Well, this was the Saturday night. Next day, Sunday, there she is hosing the car down—then off she goes. Out all day, rings Thea up to tell her not to bother with lunch or dinner, sick-visiting, she says . . . Come Sunday night Thea thinks she hears her, looks out of her window, sees Heather bringing Mrs. Abbott's car back. Leaves it in front of the house, puts the keys through the letter-box, and goes. Odd, thinks Thea. But then she sees Nigel Davis's Land-Rover. He picks up Heather and off they go. Which explains that. He must have followed behind to take Heather home again.

"Thea's still listening out for Mrs. Abbott. Nothing. Then about fifteen minutes after the Davises have gone a tap comes on Thea's door. Mrs. A. Just going to have a bath, she says, you can go to bed. Thea goes to bed, thinks no more about it till next morning, when there's talk of some car gone down a bank. Mrs. A says the driver escaped unhurt, and again that's that.

"But—there's no sign of her sister's car, so what did Mrs. Abbott come home in, thinks Thea. Then she finds a pair of ruined shoes and tights in the bin, and muddy clothes in the wash. It's obvious—it was Mrs. Abbott who had escaped unhurt and had to walk home in the rain. It was raining cats and dogs Sunday night."

"And she had borrowed a different car for her Sunday sick-visiting trip," Bassett said.

"Must have. It wasn't her sister's car that went down the bank. Thea thinks it was Nigel's."

"Why all the secrecy?" Bassett said.

Jill snorted. "That's what Tommy said. Proper daft, some women, make secrets out of anything." She put a tray of jam tarts in the oven, and made Bassett's mouth water by basting the meat while she was at it. "I think it was Mr. Abbott. He's OK, good as gold, but, as Thea says, he frowns on too much familiarity with the staff . . . There was a new man at the farm started tittle-tattling, but I put a stop to him. Nothing flighty about Mrs. Abbott, I told him, you can stop thinking what you're thinking before you start."

She took a biscuit out of a tin and slid it under the table to pup. "David Abbott was away for the weekend, you see. But it wasn't as if Mrs. Abbott was trying to hide anything. He saw the wreck being hauled up onto the road on the Monday morning on his way home. *He* knew, but as I say, he wouldn't have taken kindly to joking and leg-pulling by the staff."

Tommy Martin bowled in. A few seconds, and he was winking at Bassett and telling his wife, "Man says he'd go a beer." She laughed and fed him a fond look. "And I suppose you'll have to have one to keep him company."

So Bassett enjoyed a beer after all. He wasn't altogether certain he had benefited in other respects from the visit. Mrs. Abbott's car had "broken down." She had borrowed first Heather's car, and then Nigel Davis's Vauxhall. Both of which appeared to fit in with the hire and subsequent accident story.

Bassett, however, had spotted what he thought might be a flaw. It wasn't much of a flaw, but it was there.

He went twice to Davis's Garage next day, Monday. Once he drew up outside the house . . . He didn't like what he was doing. It wasn't a very kind thing to do.

But then neither was murder.

He little knew how close he was to the end of his investigations. Tomorrow would be a fateful day.

TWENTY-ONE

There was a ritual to be observed at market. Livestock was penned; a wander round to see what was on offer, a calculated guess as to what time an interesting lot would come under the hammer—then everyone would adjourn to the pub next door.

It had been known for certain parties to miss the sales altogether as a consequence.

When Bassett arrived, the ritual was well-advanced. There were faces there he knew, some he could give names to. John and Tony Stock. Bill Tyler. Reverend Willy. Tod Arkwright. Bassett waved, called, sidled off towards the pig pens. A couple of Gloucester Old Spot weaners took a shine to him. Man and piglets enjoyed each other's company for a time, and Bassett was reluctant to go, but Stan Harding was two pens down.

He moved along. "Day off, Mr. Harding?"

"Hour off." They leant over the pen side by side, elbows on the top bar, and talked farming small talk. Stan was thinking of returning to part-time farming. He'd been offered a field to rent, he said. Depended . . .

On what? His wife? But before Bassett could ask an appropriate question Stan reared his head to acknowledge a figure in the crowd, was saying, "See you," and dodging off. And Bassett found himself smiling into the face of a jolly woman who wedged herself into the space Stan had vacated. "I do *so* like pigs, don't you?"

"Love 'em," Bassett enthused, raising his hat, and making his escape. Like dogs, they showed friendliness; you wanted to take them home with you.

He located Stan, followed his progress with his eyes, lost him. Spotted Heather Davis. Thought he saw, far over, David Abbott. No sign of Alison. Or Nigel Davis.

He didn't go to the auctions. He sat on a seat in a quiet corner of the pub courtyard and lit a pipe. Watched head bend towards head for jokes, gossip, confidences to be exchanged, private deals clinched . . . Sensed eyes upon him . . . And turned his head in time to see in the periphery of his vision David Abbott's back making for the lounge door.

He was about to follow, to contrive a meeting, when another flick of the eye showed him Heather Davis standing on the pavement at the entrance to the courtyard, waiting. For whom? She saw him, turned away, rocking on the spot, turned again, and across the distance sought him out . . . Did she smile? Or was it a trick of the light? He rose, tapped out his pipe. No hurry. All the same . . . How weak a link in the chain was she? So sweet, so gentle . . . and nervous?

But when he looked up and across she was no longer alone, she was about to leave with Stan . . . No, wait. She was holding out a bunch of car keys. Bassett watched her mouth shape a dismissal, Stan hesitate; saw the look that passed between them. A fleeting look . . . Had he interpreted it correctly? Or was it again a trick of the light? Stan, the brother Heather never had. Her keeper—part-time? Suppose *she* was the woman with the Judge that night, would she have telephoned *her husband*? Or Stan?

Stan was loping off to the car park; Heather Davis started walking towards Bassett. He went slowly to meet her. *Was* she making for him, or someone behind him? Him. And she was smiling. Trying to . . . He raised his hat. "I was about to buy myself a coffee, Mrs. Davis. Would you care to join me?"

"Thank you." She dimpled. "I'd be pleased to."

"Where shall we go? The Copper Kettle? I hear they make excellent coffee." He steered her gently into the street.

They had the café to themselves. Lunch trade wouldn't begin for another hour. The owner served their order and withdrew.

Heather Davis moved her shoulders demurely. "I thought I knew what I was going to say, but it's gone, my mind's a blank."

They smiled at each other. She laughed, lifted her shoulders and lowered them. The expression on her face was haunting. God! No wonder she had every man who met her thinking he was being offered the key to the candy store.

"I saw you with Stan early on," she said. "What was he saying?"

"What were we talking about?" Bassett forgave her the rudeness. "Farming."

She nodded. "We grew up together."

Another silence, short and sweet. Then, "Your hair," Bassett said. "You've changed it." He had been going to affect approving surprise, but why pretend he'd only this second noticed. "It's lighter . . ."

"The bottle says ash-blonde. I often change my hair colour." Her lips moved upwards, stopped, dimpled.

"As once upon a time women would change their hats to give themselves a boost. As good as a tonic." Bassett shook his head lightly, and marvelled. She wasn't hiding a thing. Perhaps there was nothing to hide.

"Was that what you wanted to talk to me about?"

"*Did* I want to talk to you?" he said.

"I think so."

"Very well. I wanted to talk about two sisters, one a fairy princess, the other—shall we say less so? Let me guess. You were the fairy princess—"

"Stan told you that?" She wasn't displeased.

"Not Stan. It is true, though."

"It's true."

"And pretty girls make mistakes—"

She toyed with the spoon in her saucer, looked up. The smile had become a half-smile, the lovely eyes held a kind of plea.

Bassett rounded his eyes. "They get themselves into scrapes . . ."

"All the time," she said with a small sigh. Her mouth twitched self-admonishingly at the corners. "When they think they have at last grown up they still go and do something stupid."

She sipped coffee, placed the cup daintily on its saucer. "You know, don't you?" she said softly.

"That your sister Alison didn't smash the Carlton? Yes, I know, Mrs. Davis."

"And you know that Hugh Jeffries and I . . ." Her chin jerked up and down. "That's what Stan told you, isn't it? It has to be Stan. He never did believe me when I told him it had ended. As if it was any business of his," she said reproachfully. "I'm afraid he's like that."

She searched Bassett's face. "I wish . . . You have a kind face. I wish I could explain . . ."

"Why not try me?"

"There aren't many people who would understand why we did what we did. It was done with the best of intentions."

The road to hell was paved thus.

"I'm sure it was," Bassett said encouragingly.

"I'm not very good with words." She fidgeted hands, shoulders, mouth. She was like a child in many respects, a child endeavouring to be sophisticated, without knowing how.

"Tell it as it comes," Bassett coaxed. "I daresay it has its origins in childhood. Most things do."

"Childhood!" Heather Davis pouted. "I sometimes hated being the prettiest girl around. *Hated* it."

"Forgive me. You hated the adoration?"

She tucked in her chin to smile at his incredulity. "No, I loved that. What I hated was having my life mapped out for me. And so—I rebelled."

"And landed yourself in scrapes."

A nod. "And invariably Alison came to my rescue. I envied her in the end. I wish I was clever, like you, I would say. You're so capable, so feet-on-the-ground . . . I said the same thing on my wedding-day. I'm going to make an abominable wife, I said; all I am is a pretty face . . . Do you know what Alison said to that? Nonsense, she said, you're off to a good start, Heather; all you do have to do is learn to cook and use a duster. Me—I have the harder task, I have to learn to be beautiful . . . Wasn't that sweet of her? And when she was beautiful, I destroyed her self-confidence . . ."

Bassett waited.

It came. "I think she might have married Hugh Jeffries if it hadn't been for me. I thought she was cooling off . . . he was unhappy, but . . ." A pause, a short one, and a change of subject. "So you see, when she was in trouble—the one time in her life she asked me to do anything for her, I'd have been a fine sister, wouldn't I, if I had turned her down. I jumped at the opportunity to make amends. Do you see?"

"Yes, I see." He was beginning to.

"It was so *stupid,* I see that now. So very stupid. But it was all my fault, Mr. Bassett. You must believe me. I talked Nigel into helping Alison out of a jam. He wouldn't have done it otherwise."

Her mouth trembled. Bassett looked away. No tears, please, he willed her. When next she spoke it was matter-of-factly. "What do we do now, Mr. Bassett?"

Go to the police, he wanted to say.

Instead, "Your husband," he said slowly. "I'll need to speak to him, to get the whole story. Is he here?"

"At the market? No. I came in with Stan. Stan will be picking me up later. I've some calls to make."

"Does your husband know you had it in mind to talk to me like this?"

"I didn't know I was going to bump into you. But he's a bundle of nerves; he'll be glad when I tell him."

Chuffed to death, thought Bassett.

"You will be able to help us?"

Bassett smiled into the sad but somehow still dancing eyes of Heather, the pretty'un. *It was all my fault . . . I talked Nigel into helping Alison out of a jam . . .* A moment, then he took out a pen, wrote on the back of the Copper Kettle receipt. "You have my telephone number. That's my address. I should be free from six-thirty."

Bassett told Bob Greenaway on the telephone, "The Davises are coming to see me tonight, I hope. I think they may confess to insurance fraud, Bob."

"Which will help us how?" Bob said cheerfully. "Or are you speaking cryptically?"

"Not cryptically. As to how it will help us—once we get something down in black and white we have a lever. It's a start.

Tell me—has the fact that the Judge was murdered been released to the media yet?"

Answer: no. County police were keeping it under wraps for the time being. Which suited Bassett. That also might be a useful lever. There was one person at least sweating over "suspicious death," sweating on whether or not a coroner would decide in favour of murder.

Bassett spoke to Andy Miller while he was on. "Any more on Stan Harding or David Abbott?" he asked.

Nothing much. Stan was living a bachelor existence. Abbott often went away on golfing weekends. Mrs. Abbott rarely accompanied him.

TWENTY-TWO

"Heather says you're not satisfied about Mrs. Abbott's accident claim," Nigel Davis began charily. "I can't understand why, after all this time."

"Unfortunately, Mr. Davis," Bassett said as he lowered himself into his big leather armchair, "no one knew until recently that Mr. Jeffries was involved."

They were in his parlour, the french windows open, a psychological escape route. Heather Davis was wearing the same pale tweed suit she had worn in the morning, husband Nigel was in sports jacket and flannels; and only a faint shadow around the eyes and how they sat, he perched on the edge of the settee, legs astride, she beside him, sideways on, unrelaxed, let you know that underneath the cool exteriors they were apprehensive.

"I see no point in beating about the bush," Bassett said, "so I'll come straight out with it. Mr. Jeffries did hire the Vauxhall Carlton on the day you say he cancelled. He did collect the car, did drive it away." His tone was mildly reproving.

Silence. Heather Davis glanced nervously at husband Nigel,

who reached for her hand, squeezed it, received a look from her which said, it'll be all right—and nodded. "Yes, Jeffries took it," he affirmed with a sigh.

"And he bumped it."

"And he bumped it." Another nod. "He was late, and I was pushed for time. What with one thing and another—he forgot to sign the proposal form. Which meant he wasn't fully insured. I had this phone call, he'd had an accident, I got there and he'd done a bunk, leaving me to foot the bill, so—" He shrugged, not really carelessly.

"So what, Mr. Davis?"

"So I submitted a claim. An alternative claim. I couldn't see that it mattered quite honestly who had been driving the car. It's the damage that counts."

"You submitted a claim in Mrs. Abbott's name. Why Mrs. Abbott? Why not yourself, on the garage policy?"

"Because that carries an Excess clause. Any claim on that policy, I have to pay the first two hundred pounds. Add higher premiums, a possible reduced No-Claims and so on, and it would have cost me a pretty penny. All for the sake of a signature."

"If your wife had been driving—?" Bassett flicked a smile towards Heather. "Or had pretended to be—?"

"The same."

"You had Mrs. Abbott put her name to the claim form purely for financial reasons, so that you wouldn't be out of pocket. Is that what you are saying? . . . Who notified you when Mr. Jeffries had this bump?"

"Someone phoned."

"Someone. Not Mr. Jeffries."

"I don't know who it was. We'd been out for a meal, hadn't long got home. I sat down, switched on TV and dozed off. The phone woke me up. I was half-asleep."

"And so didn't recognize the voice . . . But this was the Saturday night."

"Yes."

"You go out," Bassett said slowly, "find the Carlton and bring it in. Take it out the following night. Affect a different accident in a different place. *Why?*"

"It wasn't a different accident—" Davis began.

"Oh, come on, Mr. Davis. In the genuine accident the Vauxhall hit a tree. Evidence of the fact remains to this day."

"All right. Technically I suppose you'd call it two accidents."

"One genuine, one fake," Bassett said. "Why was it necessary to fake an accident to go with Mrs. Abbott's claim?"

"I told you. Jeffries wasn't insured."

"But why *fake* an accident?" Bassett said patiently.

"I figured I had to. It had to look right—the claim form, the paperwork."

"But why?" Bassett persisted. "I'm flummoxed. You had the top copy cover-note, presumably recovered from the wrecked Carlton. Instead of sending it in to confirm a cancellation why not use it for Mrs. Abbott? Why not scrap the proposal form Hugh Jeffries neglected to sign, have Mrs. Abbott sign a fresh one, give her the cover-note—which since it carried no client's name could have been used by anyone for the specified period—and pretend that *she* had hired the car that Saturday."

Davis shook his head. "It wasn't that simple."

"Seems simple to me," Bassett said openly. "Makes more sense than pussy footing round the countryside two nights running with a smashed-up car on your back. Hell of a risk you were taking . . . You do understand what I'm getting at? If a fake accident *claim* had to be made—why not claim on the genuine accident?"

"Just switch paperwork, you mean?"

"Yes. You said it yourself—you didn't think it mattered *who* . . ."

Davis shrugged. "I left it too late. It was Sunday morning before it dawned on me I'd been lumbered."

Bassett nodded. "You said that before. Words to the effect. Jeffries had done a bunk, was how I think you put it. I confess once more to being puzzled. How could you have reached that conclusion so rapidly? Mr. Jeffries was not with the car; fair enough. But he might have staggered off, collapsed in a ditch, a field. Suffered concussion. December. Freezing cold. He could have been dying of exposure. Yet we know you didn't contact a hospital or the police; if you had, the police would have had something to go on when he was reported missing."

"You forget," Nigel Davis said. A second's smugness. "Someone phoned. I took it he was with them, being taken care of."

"In which case," Bassett said quietly, "he could have turned up at your garage on the Monday morning to sort out the accident details. You didn't wait to find out. I fear you jumped to conclusions too quickly."

Mrs. Davis had been gazing out of the windows, now and then tilting her nose as if to catch the scent of lilacs, the often stronger scent of wild thyme, but for the most part she had been motionless, listening without appearing to. Now she turned her head, mouth open to speak. Her husband spoke first.

"Look," he addressed Bassett, "I've admitted doing an insurance fiddle. What more do you want? I thought it was why you'd asked us here and not to the office—to work something out. If the insurance company want their money back, if we can do a deal . . . Heather said you could help us."

There was an edge to his voice that wasn't lost on Bassett. He spread his hands. "I am trying to help you, Mr. Davis. Tell me, where was your wife when you received the telephone call?"

"Heather? In the kitchen. Upstairs. I don't know. Upstairs, I think, or she'd have answered the phone. We don't plug in the bedroom extension until we go to bed."

"She was in the house, though. You answered the telephone. What then?"

"I went out."

"As you were?"

"No." A think. "I was wearing a good suit. I swapped into

slacks and sweater, grabbed a jacket, told Heather I had to go out—"

"Heather didn't go with you?"

"On a breakdown? Why should she?"

"You went out alone. Leaving your wife upstairs. Can you recall what you were doing, Mrs. Davis?"

She wrinkled her nose. "Struggling out of my evening dress. It was pinching."

"You had been out for the evening. A dress-up occasion. Hairdo. Wig maybe? False eyelashes—?"

"Yes!" She might have been saying: "How clever of you!"

"You see," Bassett said slowly, "I can prove you were at the scene of the genuine accident, Mrs. Davis. You left behind a tiny piece of evidence."

"My nail?" She held out and waggled the fingers of one hand. "I broke an artificial nail." She smiled. "But I could have done that any time. It *was* our car . . ."

"You didn't though, did you?" Bassett flicked eyebrows at her. "You broke your nail that night."

She moved her mouth, her shoulders, like a little girl caught out. So naïve.

"And of course Mr. Jeffries wasn't only a customer," Bassett said, turning to address her husband once more. "Your wife knew him years ago."

"Heather?" Davis's head swivelled. "What have you been *say*ing?"

"Nothing I didn't already know," Bassett said. But there was nothing to mend between them: Nigel Davis was perplexed but not angry, certainly not angry with Heather.

"You understand what I'm getting at?" Bassett went on. "You cancelled Mr. Jeffries's hire booking, you removed the Carlton from the scene of the genuine accident. In fact, by the time you had finished, *that* accident might never have been. You nullified it. Wiped it out. And in the process wiped out Mr. Jeffries's very existence . . . No accident—no Judge. Mr. Jeffries left Hereford—and vanished. Do you understand?"

Nigel Davis stared. "I'm beginning to understand what it looks like." There was a catch in his voice.

Bassett nodded. "A conspiracy, Mr. Davis. You, your wife, and Mrs. Abbott."

"It wasn't planned, for God's sake!" The colour had drained from Nigel Davis's cheeks. "All we did was juggle the insurance—"

It was Heather, her face now reflecting her husband's strain, who put it into words: "Conspiracy! You make it sound as if—as if—"

As if the whole thing had been plotted from start to finish?

"I think we'd better start again, don't you?" Bassett's tone was not unkind. "The truth this time."

The telephone rang in the hall. Bassett rose to go and answer it. "I'll make some coffee while I'm at it. I'm sure you would like a cup, I know I would." Thus he let them know they had some time to themselves.

He paused at the door. "Incidentally, Mr. Davis—I found your wife's broken nail *inside the cottage.*" Paused after opening the door. "Also, I cannot conceive of a woman in Mrs. Abbott's position agreeing to participate in insurance fraud merely to save you a few hundred pounds. We both know there's more to it than that. So think carefully. Don't leave her out, eh?"

He made a face to add emphasis, pulled the door shut behind him, peeped at pup asleep in the kitchen, picked up the receiver, and listened to Bob Greenaway.

"Davises turn up?"

"They're here now."

"Any joy?"

"I think so. Stay near the telephone, Bob. I'll be in touch."

TWENTY-THREE

"It was I who had the phone call about Hugh," Heather Davis said, embarking on their story. "We had been out for the evening, as Nigel said. We'd been home about twenty minutes when Nigel was called out, a driver who'd run out of petrol, so I was on my own when Alison rang up about ten minutes later. She said she was with Hugh and they'd had an accident. Nothing serious, but it meant she was stuck, could I go and pick her up.

"When I got there—just up the lane, it was—I was quite shocked. It wasn't the slight accident Alison made out; they'd hit a tree, bashed in the front end, and Hugh was hurt and Alison looked *awful.* I wanted to get Nigel on the car radio, tell him to fetch a doctor or ambulance, but Hugh said no. He was adamant. His main concern was for Alison to get away. What were a few injuries, he said, compared to what some newspapers would make of him and Alison if they got hold of the story. I couldn't see how the papers would get to know, but Hugh said there was always someone ready to crawl from behind a bush and tip them off.

"He wanted Alison to take my car and go, there and then. But Alison refused. Hugh was still in the Carlton and she wasn't budging until he was well clear. She kept on about it catching fire or exploding. She'd thought Hugh was getting out of the Carlton when she went to phone me—at one of the cottages, I think, further up the lane—and she was horrified to find him still in the car when she got back. I realized, even if she didn't, that he must have felt worse than he said. I don't think he could get out, not on his own—"

"Did he say anything about having tried?"

"No, but I think he might have done. He said his chest pained him, and he thought he'd broken his leg; but Alison was to get clear, and then we could worry about him. But Alison's like a leech once she's made up her mind. She wouldn't go until Hugh was safe.

"In the end he agreed to let us help him to that cottage. We couldn't take him in my car because it was pointed in the wrong direction. I'd have had to drive on a fair distance to turn round, and there'd be noise and activity and—anyway, we could be there, Hugh said, while we were messing about.

"Which was true. We got him out of the Carlton, and sort of half-cradled him—Alison knew what to do—and got him to the cottage. Alison still wouldn't leave, she had to make him comfortable, as if I were an idiot. We put the gas fire on, and Alison was going to get a gas lamp, but I had a flashlamp—one of those big square ones. Hugh said that would do, and, well, Alison agreed eventually to go.

"We went to my car, I radioed Nigel, then I gave her the keys. She drove off, and I went back to poor Hugh. Cracked a rib or two, I think, he said. I told him that Alison should have made a 999 call . . . She could have, you know"—to Bassett, shifting the onus of blame onto her sister—"Alison could have dialled 999 and then started walking, found a phone box to call me . . .

"Anyway"—hands fluttering—"Hugh disagreed. Patience, Heather, he kept saying. Get that man of yours to shift the Carlton; we'll take it from there. I suppose it was because he was a judge—and Alison was married—and also he'd had a few drinks. That might have bothered him—if they'd breathalysed him. The tabloids would have a field day, he said, if the mood was upon them.

"Well, then he closed his eyes. I thought he'd passed out, but he hadn't, he had a headache to cap everything else. If he hadn't spoken I'd never have left him, but he was joking even with his eyes closed; telling me about the number of times he'd been to the cottage and hadn't seen another vehicle, but with his luck a fleet would turn up tonight. He wanted me to go and watch the Carlton, to make sure nothing bashed into it. So I went and did as he said. About five minutes later Nigel arrived."

Nigel Davis took up the tale from there. "I wasn't far away when Heather got me on the radio. On my road home, actually. I headed for here instead."

Bassett nodded. "You were already in a recovery vehicle."

"The Land-Rover, yes. That time of night I go prepared. When folk say they've run out of petrol they most times have, but now and then, especially on Saturday nights, if they've had a few drinks—could be anything."

Heather was agitated, he said, nearly had him running to see Jeffries there and then. But he thought it best to do as the man wanted. The man knew how he felt. Say ten minutes at most to free the Carlton, and then they could all be heading for warmth and a bed, Jeffries as well. They could drop him off at the hospital if he wished.

"That's what we did, attended to the Carlton first. Not a big job, drag the Carlton off, suspend the front end, job done, mobile . . . Got to the cottage. Heather stayed with the Land-Rover while I went in. He was dead."

Heather again: "Nigel was only in about a minute. He came out hardly able to speak. I couldn't believe it when he told me. Hugh *couldn't* be dead."

"You saw—?"

"No. But Nigel—" Nigel had told her.

Bassett nodded, addressed her husband. "You're sure Hugh Jeffries was dead?"

"No pulse, no heartbeat," he said knowledgeably.

"Nigel's done First-Aid courses," Heather Davis said.

"Right-o. You found the man dead. What next?"

Sheer blind panic. There they were—dead body on their hands, proof of a road accident hooked onto the Land-Rover, no police notified, no ambulance. Afterwards they bitterly regretted having panicked, but at the time, in the dead of night, everything they had done having been enshrouded in secrecy— and it was pitch black all round them, eerie all of a sudden, making everything seem worse—they felt dirty, guilty as hell, saw their actions as being furtive, and were convinced the police would think so too. They weren't going to stop and find out. The impulse was to run.

"Also there was Alison," Heather said.

It was Alison Heather wanted to protect first and foremost, and there was no hope of explaining their actions without bringing Alison into it—the very thing Hugh had sought desperately to avoid. Protecting Alison's reputation was imperative.

"She'd been so good to me in the past . . . Her *one* mistake. I couldn't let her down. I talked Nigel into leaving everything . . ."

Not then, no; not while they were at the cottage. *Then* they couldn't get away fast enough. The talking, most of it, took place after they were home; when they debated what they had done, what they ought to have done . . . what Alison should have done at the very beginning. Alison *could* have summoned help for Hugh and then vanished into the darkness, never mind what Hugh demanded.

They had sat up all night discussing ways of letting the police know that Hugh was in the cottage. But always there was Alison to consider. Every move they made was with Alison in mind. If it hadn't been for Alison . . .

Bassett began to understand why Mrs. Abbott had agreed to her part in the insurance fraud.

"May we return for a minute to when you found Hugh dead, Mr. Davis. You told your wife. And then—?"

"I had to go back to switch off the fire and collect Heather's flashlamp."

"Which took you how long?"

"A couple of minutes. I checked again to make sure he was dead."

"Did you lock the door behind you?"

There was no key in the lock, the garage owner said. "I thought Hugh must have it in his pocket. I didn't dare go and look." He had the jitters by then. "Heather told me afterwards that Alison had put the key on the kitchen table on her way out."

Heather: "Alison said it was a habit of theirs never to leave the key on the outside. It—she probably did it automatically."

It made sense, and if true disposed of the key as a puzzle. The Davises weren't in a hurry to lock the dead man in; their concern was to get the hell out of the mess they were in as fast as they could.

"Continue from when you arrived home . . ."

They locked the Land-Rover and wrecked Carlton safely out of sight in the garage workshop for the whole of the Sunday; they didn't open even for petrol on Sundays. Then they sat talking.

They continued talking now. Bassett noted every inflection in their voices, every pause, every word left unspoken. In his imagination he followed them through that fateful night, heard fear evaporate, indignation take its place . . . Why should they have all the worry? Nothing to do with them! All they had done was recover a damaged car. Sod it! put a claim in for the Carlton! Why should they be out of pocket? OK, so they couldn't put a claim in for Jeffries—so let Alison do her bit!

Gradually, without them actually saying as much, it came to Bassett that by dawn the Davises had decided—and continued to believe—that they had done nothing wrong; that the plan for Alison to have the "accident" on Sunday night was perfectly legitimate; that they were the true injured parties in the affair.

Heather explained it beautifully: "After all, there had been an accident. It wasn't as if we were claiming for something that never happened. And if we had gone to the police on Sunday, which we did think of doing once, the insurance company could have suspected the delay and used it to wriggle out. And anyway, Alison's claim would be foolproof. She would be in the clear. Which was Hugh's dying wish, when all was said and done."

Nothing surprised Bassett. In a lifetime of bobbying he had seen and heard it all.

"I suppose we *have* to go to the police now?"

"It would be wise," he advised levelly. "Better than having them come to you."

"Now? Tonight, do you think?"

Most certainly. While the urge was upon them to set the record straight. For that was all they thought they were doing. They had made a foolish mistake: they fled. From then on matters had grown out of control. They were victims of circumstance. Fraud, conspiracy to defraud, failure to report an accident, failure to report a death, concealing evidence—mention these and they would surely be horrified. You can't charge us with those! Why us?

Why us? Wounded innocents.

If he were to add *murder* to the list . . . ?

He often felt like weeping for the frailties and deficiencies of that poor weak animal, the human being, but—*murder*. He stifled anger.

"Tonight, yes, Mrs. Davis." Tonight their major crime was lack of common decency. By tomorrow they might have changed their minds about what they had just told him. By all means tonight. Get it down in black and white.

"Do you mind if I ask you one or two questions first? What time was it when your sister rang you up? Roughly."

"After midnight. Half past or thereabouts."

The time fitted the blonde woman's call from Brown Owl Cottage.

"What were you wearing when you left your house?"

"Oh, gosh. Trousers. My jacket, I think. Yes, my white hooded jacket. I always wear that when I go out in the dark. Nigel has one of those orange ones."

"Your sister?"

"What was she wearing?"

"Mm. Blue dress?"

"No, it was red, I think. And she was wearing a black hooded cape coat. Black fashion boots . . ."

"What about her hair?"

"She had the hood up. Oh, you mean—yes, I think she had on a blonde wig. She got the idea from me, I often wear party wigs."

"Does Alison? Or did she only wear a wig when she went out with Hugh?"

"I don't really know. I didn't know she was seeing Hugh, I mean. Not until that night."

Bassett regarded her thoughtfully for a moment, then: "Just one more, then I'll let you go. When you left the house to go to your sister, did anyone see you leave?"

Nigel Davis looked puzzled, as well he might. But Heather Davis saw nothing wrong with the question. "Stan might have," she said. "He lives opposite, and I'm sure I saw him at the window when I got my car out. I remember because I thought: oh God! there'll be a post-mortem in the morning and he'll be cracking his unfunny jokes: where were you sneaking off to late last night? He's getting to be a proper old woman since his wife left him. Tedious." She scowled. "But we didn't see him all day Sunday. He must have forgotten it by Monday."

"Said nothing to me," Nigel Davis murmured.

"I'm sure he'll remember, though, if you ask him," Heather Davis said sweetly.

"Right." Bassett returned her smile. "I'll let you go. Ask for Inspector Robert Greenaway. I'll give him a tinkle, shall I?" He looked at Nigel Davis. "Tell him to expect you."

He waited until he heard them drive away, then he reached for the telephone.

"They've just left, Bob. Don't frighten them. Sit them down and take their statements. I think they'll talk freely. They knew this day would come: they've rehearsed their side of the story so often they could tell it in their sleep. I'll be down within the hour."

•   •   •   •

During that hour Bassett took Tod Arkwright's route to Crum Cottage. Using his own key as before, he let himself in; whispered mischievously, "Are you there, Tabitha?" but was immensely grateful when there was no reply. As he went through to where Judge Jeffries's body had been found, the picture was clearer now. He could see the two sisters here, and a flesh and blood man anxious to preserve Alison's reputation—as well as his own. He could imagine the man making light of his injuries to Heather Davis, and perhaps laughing and joking about them, as she had said.

"Poor old lad," he murmured.

The chair in which the Judge had been sitting had been moved. He pushed it back into its position, sat down in the chair opposite, and lit a pipe. An earlier threatening rain cloud had passed over, there was a bright orange sun setting; the room was cool and shaded where Bassett sat, the window and shelves at the far end of the room limned by the evening glow. A not unpleasant place to sit and ponder.

He visualized Hugh Jeffries sitting across from him, his forehead marked by the blow received when he hit the windscreen . . . ruminated on Heather's recounting of events that fateful night . . . conjectured on the killer entering and aiming a blow. *The* blow.

When the pipe had been smoked, he stood up. He had seen what he came to see.

Jeffries's murderer was right-handed. There was insufficient room between the fireplace and the armchair for a left-handed killer to have aimed a forceful blow.

He closed the door softly behind him, turned the key, and walked slowly down the path, remembering Stan Harding and his dicky finger.

TWENTY-FOUR

"The Abbott woman won't play ball," was how Inspector Bob Greenaway greeted Bassett at the station.

"Turned down your invitation, eh?" Alison Abbott had been requested to help the police—her sister and husband were to have been the hook—"They are currently making statements" —but Alison didn't want to know. She had had an accident, had followed the proper procedure, and that was an end of it. Finish. "We shouldn't be surprised," Bassett said. "A legal secretary—she knows her rights."

He and the inspector had met in an upstairs corridor. Bassett followed Bob into his office. "How far have the Davises got?"

"Statements are being typed. They're tucking into tea and sandwiches at the moment. I did as you suggested, let it flow. Simple, isn't it, when you know."

"You believe them?"

"Don't you?"

Bassett nodded. "I do. It has a distinct ring of truth about it. And it's feasible. Even to the running away." He moved his shoulders expressively. "Put most folk in their shoes . . ."

"It makes sense," Bob said grudgingly. "As far as it goes. I made one or two notes, bearing in mind that it's murder we're chasing, even if they don't know that."

He looked at his papers. "The husband goes into the cottage alone after they hooked up the Carlton. Comes out: the Judge is dead. Goes back in: about two minutes. I say he goes in, sees Jeffries asleep, returns to his wife, *says* Jeffries is dead, she's to stay where she is. Goes back in, picking up a rock on the way—"

"Motive?" Bassett asked.

"Satisfaction. No man, I don't care how daft he is, shuts his eyes completely to his wife's carryings-on. Andy's been telling me a few things."

"You think that out of all of Heather's menfriends he chose Jeffries?"

"Symbolic," Bob Greenaway said. "The opportunity presented itself. He'd been wanting to wallop one of her paramours for a long time. Jeffries was it. Davis felt a whole lot better for it. Restored his manhood."

"It's a theory," Bassett conceded.

"Right, what else? Yes, radio. Mrs. Davis says she radioed her husband from her car. I wondered about that. Jeffries had Mr. Davis's car: was there a radio in it? I was thinking of that telephone call: why telephone if you have a radio? But Davis said he took his radio out before he let Jeffries have the car . . . Jeffries's BMW. They say they didn't know he came to Glevebourne in his BMW. At a guess the murderer didn't know about it either, or he'd have done something about losing it . . . Mrs. D described what her sister was wearing. She said you'd asked her, so she thought I'd like to know too—"

Bob Greenaway interrupted himself. "Are they real?" he said quizzically. "They're so half-soaked, dropping everybody in it, right, left and centre; including themselves!"

"More to be pitied than blamed, you mean."

Bob screwed up his face. "They don't think they've done any wrong, do they? She was telling the tale as if it had just happened, and they were reporting it as they ought to have done eighteen months ago."

Bassett grinned. "You're getting grey hairs, Bob." It was the nearest he could get to commiserating. "What else have you got down there?"

"Nothing useful. My suspicious nature at work. Mrs. Davis says her affair with Jeffries ended long ago. She could be lying. Or Mr. D could have thought she was lying. Question: was *she* out with Jeffries, husband follows and forces them off the road? Link that to her telling me what her sister was wearing. It could have been *she* who was wearing the red dress and black cloak. Who's to say it wasn't? But that's where that comes unstuck. If just the two of them were involved, why implicate the Abbott woman, et cetera, et cetera . . . My last note reads: who nipped in during the ten minutes they spent hooking up the wreck? Ample time for someone, Harry. Unless, as I say, Davis did the clobbering himself."

"Do they know they've been ditched by Mrs. Abbott?" Bassett inquired.

"No. Thought I'd wait." An eyebrow went up. "Think she might have a change of heart?"

"We could give her a nudge," said Bassett. "Make a suggestion, Bob? Let me go. I've met the lady . . . But I'd like to say hello to the Davises first, if I may."

They were in an interview room downstairs. Sergeant Andy Miller was just leaving. "Is there a constable in there, Andy? If he wants a tea-break . . . I'll probably need ten minutes. Bob's OK'd it."

Andy called the constable out. "Not looking too good for the Smiths, guvnor. From where I've been sitting, it still looks as if they could have been lying in wait and bumped him off at the first opportunity."

"Someone did, Andy. Someone did. Do me a favour? Give me five minutes, then fetch Nigel Davis. Can do?"

"Can do."

They seemed pleased to see him. It was a stark room, as interview rooms usually are. But: "Not as bad as I thought it might be," was Heather's reply to Bassett's inquiry if they were being looked after. Nigel Davis was quiet, heavy-eyed, but far from morose. He wasn't too keen on the bars on the windows, but otherwise had no complaints.

"I know you must be tired," Bassett said, "but would you mind clarifying one or two points for me. Mrs. Davis, when your sister drove off in your car, where was she aiming for?"

"Home."

"Her own home, or yours?" He was thinking of what Jill Martin had told him: Alison turned up in Heather's car on the

Saturday night. But—her own car—surely she had rendez-voused with Hugh Jeffries . . .

Heather Davis might have been reading his mind. "Her own home . . . Oh! You're thinking about her car. She'd left it in town. On one of those Pay and Display parks. She said Hugh used to pick her up from there . . . That was in winter, dark nights. In summer they would meet in a country lane . . . That night she could have gone for her own car and left mine in its place, but she would have had to leave the keys inside. We decided she should go straight home, and any questions asked she had broken down, I had lent her my car, and Nigel would "fix" hers next day."

"Questions asked by Mr. Abbott?" Jill had said David was away.

But Mrs. Davis had it. "By anybody. I don't think David was there. I was to take her car to the farm and bring mine back. Or Nigel would have done it. One of us. Of course by Sunday morning everything had changed."

Instead of delivering Alison's car to her they rang her up, broke the news gently that Hugh was dead, and told her not to worry, they had a foolproof plan.

"She came straightaway. In my car. Afterwards she phoned her housekeeper to say she would be out all day, on a mercy mission, and then she spent the day with us. She was dreadfully upset, so she was better off with us, in any case."

And her absence from home would lend credence to the car-hire tale should there ever be a query.

In fact, everything they did on that Sunday was geared to fit the car-hire story. Alison stayed with them, out of sight. Heather fetched Alison's Volvo from town and Nigel tinkered with it. Then late on the Sunday night—it was foul weather, cold and wet, hardly anyone about, so they didn't have to leave it too late—Alison went with Nigel in the Land-Rover, the Carlton on its back; Heather followed in Alison's Volvo . . . They made sure no one saw them leave the garage. No one meaning Stan. And once on the main road, who would look twice at a smashed-up car being transported by a recovery vehicle?

The Carlton was unhooked and sent down the bank. Heather delivered the Volvo to the farm. She left it in front of the house, a note on the seat: "Fixed. Should be OK now." Nigel picked her up in the Land-Rover—an unencumbered Land-Rover by this time. Meanwhile, Alison stood in the rain getting soaked, mussed herself up—and when the Davises were well clear let herself into the house. The idea was for Alison to behave as if she had been in the "accident" but not to advertise the fact. She made sure the housekeeper would find her ruined shoes and muddy clothes, but at the same time said not a thing.

And it worked. Everybody knew it was Mrs. Abbott who had had the accident, she attracted a certain amount of silent sympathy, and the incident died a quiet death, so to say. No gossip, no unwanted speculation.

Bassett turned to Nigel Davis. "Does Stan Harding have a radio in his car?"

Davis frowned. "Yes . . ."

"Back to you, Mrs. Davis. Could we go through the night of Mr. Jeffries's accident one more time. What I'm attempting to do is get a picture. You were there that night, you experienced it, it's all up here—" tapping his head. "Me? I couldn't even tell you what the weather was like. You've told me it was cold and wet on the Sunday. What was it doing on the Saturday?"

"Is that important?"

"It could be. It's a detail." Details were essential if he was to get at the truth. "Close your eyes and tell me what you saw as you drove up Long Lane."

As Mrs. Davis closed her eyes, Bassett glanced at her husband. Davis was watching him fixedly. Bassett looked away. "When you are ready, Mrs. Davis."

"A tunnel," she said. "Which seemed to go on for an age. Frost on the trees and grass. I remember thinking that if the heater wasn't working in the car they'd be so *cold* . . . I slowed when I reached the cottage, but it was in total darkness so I carried on up. That's right—that was when I thought of the cold. I thought of them standing by the Carlton shivering, I ought to have brought a flask of soup . . . My headlights picked up the Carlton as a pale smudge. No sign of them. Then the Carlton properly . . . Yes, for a second I thought it was just parked, no lights on, then I saw the front end, it had hit a tree. I drove right up . . . managed to squeeze round it—and pulled up behind." She opened her eyes. "How did I do?"

Bassett smiled. "Excellently." That last sentence fitted in with what George Tipper had seen. "You said you slowed when you reached the cottage. You knew about the cottage, then—?"

"Alison told me when she phoned. She said that was where they might be."

"You didn't know previously?"

"That she and Hugh went there? No."

"But you did know Alison was seeing Hugh Jeffries."

She glanced at her husband. "No, I didn't."

"You didn't put two and two together when Hugh hired cars from you?"

"No!" She laughed, at herself, for the oversight. "I suppose it did occur to me perhaps once. But it was so obvious. Too obvious. Of course I realized afterwards that Alison might have put Hugh up to it. If she ever *was* spotted in one of our hire cars she could always talk her way out of it by saying she was giving Nigel a hand, delivering or collecting, or something. Clever of her, wasn't it?"

"Very," Bassett said drily.

Andy Miller chose that moment to fetch Nigel Davis.

"To sign your statement, Mr. Davis—"

The door closed behind them.

"Why only Nigel?" Heather Davis wanted to know. A worry frown had sprouted. "Why couldn't we both go?"

"Your turn next, I daresay." Bassett smiled reassuringly. "So I'd better hurry up. A quick recap, if I may. You and your sister left the cottage together after you'd seen that Mr. Jeffries was as comfortable as possible." He gave her a swift, different kind of smile. "You do mean together. Alison didn't hold back and join up with you at the gate, or—"

"Oh no. Together."

"You radioed your husband; Alison left in your car. You returned to the cottage alone. Spent a few minutes with Mr. Jeffries . . . He had a gas fire to warm him, a flashlamp to provide light . . . Did you close the curtains?"

Andy re-entered the room and went to sit in a chair in the corner.

"The curtains?" Heather Davis said. She shook her head. "I don't know. I don't remember."

She was looking tired now, even her voice was weary.

"Nearly through, Mrs. Davis. I have to ask you this, it is rather important. In retrospect—think carefully—were you aware of anything that might suggest you were not alone—that you were being followed?"

Followed? *Followed?*

The frown was back. "When I first arrived, you mean? A vehicle?" Also the headshake. "I don't think there was anything behind me. There couldn't have been, or it would have passed us. Or . . ." The frown deepened. "It could have stopped, couldn't it? I . . ." She shook her head again, bewildered. "Somewhere lower down. On that stretch of grass just below the cottage . . ."

Bassett nodded. "A car parked there without lights."

"Yes." She stared. "I wouldn't have seen it."

"When Alison drove off—which direction did she take?"

"She carried on up the lane and out the top end."

"And from which direction did your husband arrive?"

"From the top—"

"Driving down the lane."

"Yes."

"So if there had been a vehicle parked lower down, neither Alison leaving nor your husband arriving would have seen it."

"No . . . But we'd have passed it—Nigel and I—in the

Land-Rover, on our way out. We left that way." Her eyes were troubled. "Unless . . ."

"Unless," Bassett said, appearing to finish for her, "it had gone by then."

She searched his face.

"Meanwhile you returned to the Carlton to wait for your husband. Did you hear him—or any vehicle—before he actually arrived, Mrs. Davis?"

"No." Once more the slow headshake.

"But then he did arrive, and the two of you prised the Carlton off the tree and hooked it up . . . Hugh Jeffries was on his own for ten minutes."

It took a moment. "At least ten minutes, Mr. Bassett. I must have been standing in the lane for all of five or six minutes before Nigel came."

"I see."

A short silence fell.

At last they were smiling at each other. "I think that will do, Mrs. Davis. Thank you for your help."

He stood up. "By the way, who thought out the fake accident? You—when you were talking your husband into protecting your sister?" Bassett made it sound like casual curiosity, with a promise of praise for the one with the brains.

"Me?" Heather Davis said. "Good heavens, no! It was Nigel who worked all that out." All Nigel's work.

Andy Miller followed Bassett out. "I think Davis has got an idea that the sister-in-law has denied all knowledge."

"Could be," Bassett agreed abstractedly.

Andy snapped his fingers. "Penny for them."

"Eh? Oh, sorry. I was thinking, Andy. About the lady. For a moment in there . . ." He turned to face the young sergeant. "She doesn't know that *we* know it's murder." His gaze was reflective now. "Perhaps . . . Yes. Methinks therein lies the answer."

Andy waggled his eyebrows. Was he supposed to comprehend what Bassett was talking about? He waited. But Bassett merely glanced out at the night sky as they passed a corridor window and said, "I'd best be off. Early to bed, early to rise, they say, don't they, farmers? I'm off to see the Abbotts before they go to bed."

TWENTY-FIVE

The Abbotts' house was flooded with light. God's in his heaven, all's right with the world! Or were they lights of defiance? The police?—they can go to hell! Party spirit, that's the thing: bung them all on! show them we don't give a toss! There was indeed soft music floating out of an upstairs window.

But no party going on. The master and his wife were spending a quiet evening at home. Alison Abbott herself, in classically simple sapphire blue, answered his thumb-press on the doorbell. Bassett had wondered how they could receive him, if they *would* receive him—they didn't have to, they could have told him to go to hell. But she was charming, as ever.

"Come in, Inspector!" she invited with a flourish. "No, it was an inspector I spoke to on the telephone. Greenaway was his name? You are Mr. Bassett," She held her hand out to take his hat. "Same errand, no doubt. You have come from the police station?"

"Oh yes," Bassett replied truthfully.

One swift, all-seeing look took in a hall whose rugs would have fitted the rooms in his cottage wall-to-wall, wood panelling, paintings, elegant jardinieres, beautiful staircase . . . and two spaniels come to sticky-beak from the room whose door Alison had left ajar.

"This way—" She waved a hand. From within the room a voice called lustily to the dogs: "Jasper! Thomas!"

"Your husband, Mrs. Abbott? Is there somewhere more private—?"

"You and I alone?" She fed him an amused tut-tut look. "That would be foolish of me, wouldn't it? Tantamount to admitting I had something to hide. Please . . ."

Please enter: the drawing-room, where David Abbott was standing in front of a Baronial Hall style fireplace, the dogs at attention by his feet. The man, not the fireplace, dominated the room. The dogs wagged their tails.

"Ah! Bassett! Had a feeling we hadn't seen the last of you." The tone sought to depreciate, the use of the surname to put Bassett in his place. Bassett, however, was accustomed to being addressed thus: it was, always had been, his choice. Nevertheless, he couldn't resist the challenge.

" 'Evening, Abbott," he said with a smile.

The other man fondled the dogs' heads until the moment had passed, then gestured. "Sit down, old man. We are drinking whisky. What will yours be?"

"I'm afraid Heather's come a cropper this time," Alison said, as drinks were poured and they all sat down.

"You've been advised of her story?"

"Oh yes. We know exactly what she's saying," Alison replied, looking at her husband for support. "And there is a limit. She has to learn to stand on her own feet."

"Hear, hear," from David Abbott. "What Alison means is that for once in her life Heather must get herself out of whatever mess she's in. Cock and bull yarn, anyway, as anyone who knows Heather would tell you. My wife running to Heather for help! You have to be joking! Boot's on the other foot, old man. Always has been. Heather's the one who's forever in trouble. Crisis after crisis, all her life."

"Mrs. Davis did tell me that," Bassett said. Turning to Alison: "She says she welcomed the opportunity to do you a favour for a change."

"Clever Heather," David Abbott rejoined. "Noble Heather too, now. Incredible! Got you sucked in, eh? Those appealing eyes and the little-girl voice."

"David, please . . ." his wife protested mildly. "You make

her sound horrid, and she's not. She's just silly," she said to Bassett.

Bassett said he understood. "Would you mind if I went through certain aspects of Mrs. Davis's story? . . . She says you rang her up . . ."

"I've been thinking about that. The night before I hired the Carlton, wasn't it? Yes, I did phone Heather. My car wouldn't start."

"Phoned from where, Mrs. Abbott?"

"A call-box in town. Nigel was out on a breakdown so Heather came herself. She managed to get the car going, but it kangarooed—I don't know the technical term—so she lent me her own car, a Nova. And she kangarooed mine to the garage."

"What were you wearing, Mrs. Abbott?"

"Great scott! You can't possibly expect me to remember after all this time!"

"Can you remember what time it was when you rang up your sister?"

"That's easier. Around midnight. A little before."

"May I ask why you didn't telephone your husband to come and fetch you?"

David Abbott said, "I wasn't here."

"I see." Bassett turned to Alison again. "What then? You had your sister's car, she had taken yours—"

"I needed transport for the whole of Sunday. Heather needed her car, too. She could have used Nigel's Carlton, but she was wary of it; it was a more powerful car than she was used to. So I returned her Nova and hired Nigel's Carlton. I did the thing properly so that I could put it through the books as expenses."

Astute! thought Bassett. He asked, "What was the arrangement? Were you to return the Carlton and pick up your repaired Volvo?"

"I don't recall that we had an arrangement," Alison said thoughtfully. "All I know is that Nigel repaired my car during

the day and brought it here on Sunday night. It was waiting for
me when I arrived home.''

"Arrived home after the accident with the Carlton?''

"Well yes, of course.''

"Did anyone see the car brought back?''

"Our housekeeper. She was listening out for me, saw
Heather leave my car, Nigel collect her in the Land-Rover.''

"Can't see anything wrong with that," David Abbott put in.
"You deliver a car, you need someone to run you back. And my
wife is speaking the truth. They left a note on one of the seats.''

"Fixed, should be OK," Bassett said. "I know about the note.
The Davises say it was all part of a plan. You say, Mrs. Abbott,
that your car genuinely needed repairs. Right-o, fair enough.
They repair your car, Heather brings it here, Nigel following in
the Land-Rover. He obviously knew you wouldn't be here to
run Heather home. I'll accept that also. What I don't comprehend is why they went to so much trouble on a cold, wet night. I
would have thought the common-sense arrangement would
have been as we said—for you to pick up the repaired Volvo
when you returned the Carlton at the end of the hire period.''

A short awkward silence ensued. David Abbott's eyes narrowed. "What are you suggesting?''

"I'm trying to get at the truth, Mr. Abbott. There appears to
be no valid reason for returning your wife's Volvo late on the
Sunday night—unless the Davises already knew the Carlton no
longer existed, and Mrs. Abbott was going to be without transport the following day.''

"Or unless they'd good reason of their own. D'you know
what I'd do if I were you, old man? I would reverse every
blasted word Heather has told me.''

Bassett seemed to give a little. "Work on the premise that it
was Heather herself who was with Jeffries that night, you
mean?''

"Got it in one," said Abbott.

"I hate to have to say it," Alison added, "but has Nigel said
he saw me or my car anywhere near the scene of this other

accident, the one in which Hugh was hurt?" She rolled her eyes, moved her body apologetically, a woman battling to be both loyal to her sister and yet fair to herself. "Who fetched Nigel to it? Not I, and he knows it."

"It was Heather," Bassett admitted quietly.

"And it was Heather who was there when Nigel arrived, again not I. I didn't see Nigel that night. My sister used me, Mr. Bassett. She wove a story around me to explain to Nigel what she was doing there. And when Hugh's body was found she had no alternative but to stick to her original explanation . . . Am I right—Heather more or less volunteered the information to the police?"

"To me," Bassett said.

A rueful smile touched the corners of Alison Abbott's lips. "I suspect she decided to get in first. After she found out where you live. What might you recall to memory of that night! She'd have had nightmares over it."

Bassett managed a half-smile also. "And she thought you would back her story?"

Alison nodded. "As no doubt Nigel does. As ever."

"Easily led, Nigel," David Abbott said boisterously. He drained his glass, made as if to rise, his attitude not impolite but clearly dismissive.

But Bassett was not to be hurried. He picked up his glass and held it without drinking. David Abbott sank down into his chair again. "Tell me, Mrs. Abbott," Bassett said. "If your sister was with you, trying to start your Volvo in Glevebourne, at midnight, how could she also have been out with the Judge?"

She was only momentarily discomfited. "I've since discovered that Hugh invariably left the car he hired on the garage forecourt and walked to the railway station . . . Take it that on that Saturday he arrived at the same time as Heather turned up with my car. Take it that Heather, knowing Nigel was out on a breakdown which might keep him occupied for an hour or so, went with Hugh for, shall we say, a spin. Hugh could be very persuasive."

Balderdash! Less strongly, Bassett could have argued: what was Hugh doing all day that he met no one who would come forward when he was reported missing? Who else had he been seeing in Glevebourne if not one of you? . . . He said nothing of the kind. He nodded. "Yes, that would be possible."

Now he finished his drink, thanked them, rose. "Alas, I remain confused," he said slowly. "Mrs. Davis says she radioed her husband from her own car. She couldn't have, though, could she? Not if she had lent her car to you, Mrs. Abbott."

"She did lend me her car, Mr. Bassett, if that is your query. My housekeeper will tell you—"

David Abbott jumped up. "Radio in Jeffries's car. Thought of that?" he asked Bassett.

"Davis removed the radio before he hired the car out. And there you have it, Mr. Abbott. The car the Judge hired—the car he crashed on the Saturday night—was Davis's own car. Traces of that accident remain in Long Lane to this day. It puzzles me . . ."

He stopped there. Alison's face. She knew what was coming. It puzzles me how you, Mrs. Abbott, came to hire a car on the Sunday that had been rendered a candidate for a scrapyard the night before. She was begging him, *begging* him not to say it.

But David Abbott was no idiot. "Don't know what you are implying now, Bassett, but I saw the Carlton myself in the gulley—"

"When was this?" Bassett feigned renewed keenness.

"On the Monday morning. Everything I saw that morning bears out my wife's story. The note on the front seat of her Volvo. The keys in the letter-box. A pair of shoes she ruined walking in the rain. Plus—I saw them winching up the Carlton. I was returning from a weekend away."

"You'd been away from when?"

"From Saturday morning. Delivering Christmas boxes to my family scattered around the Midlands."

"So you saw the Carlton being recovered," Bassett said. "You didn't see how it got into the gulley in the first place. I see." He moved towards the door. The two dogs reclining on the hearthrug lifted their heads lazily. As lazily Bassett murmured, "We had an idea the Carlton was pushed."

He smiled at Alison, held her gaze while he said with slow, low emphasis, "I don't think I've left anything behind . . ." And then they were exchanging old-fashioned courtesies. "Good evening, Mr. Bassett." A moment or so later David Abbott was showing him out.

"Good night," was all the farmer said.

Bassett did not go to his car. He began a stroll towards the rhododendrons . . . The door behind him opened: Alison, his hat in her hand. "Mr. Bassett! You forgot your hat!"

There was a laugh in the words—for her husband's benefit. As Bassett drew closer she whispered, "I'd like to talk to you. Shall we walk?" She had come prepared, a coat hung loosely from her shoulders like a cloak. "In the garden. Then if David comes I can say I'm showing you round . . . This way, there are lights around here, and a bench."

She led him round the corner of the house.

TWENTY-SIX

They walked under lamplight and stars. She was beautiful, Bassett thought, her bone structure finer than Heather's, her beauty the kind that would last far longer than her sister's. She probably never had been the ugly duckling Darcy described; more likely she hadn't made the most of herself. Or had—only no one noticed while Heather was there. Was that why she hadn't fought for Jeffries, why she had stepped back, a habit of a lifetime, and let her sister have her own way? She'd lost so many battles when young and the males all around had seen only what they had wanted to see, she hadn't the self-assurance needed to fight?

"I love my husband very much," she said now, low and

trembly. "I don't want him hurt. Do you think the insurance company would accept restitution?"

"You're admitting you took part in an insurance fraud?"

"I'm admitting nothing, Mr. Bassett. What I am doing is asking if you would offer a cheque on behalf of my brother-in-law. I should like to end it, and in my experience most insurance companies are prepared to waive legal action in certain circumstances."

They walked slowly in step. "Who are you trying to protect, Mrs. Abbott?"

"I've said. My husband. I don't want him hurt. As he will be if he learns I did anything so foolish."

"Are we still talking about the Carlton?"

"Well, of course," was her reply.

The bench was tucked in against some bushes, and lit by the glow from a lamp on a nearby wall. "Come and sit down," Bassett said gruffly, and when they were seated: "I tried to spare you back in the house, by not blabbing in front of your husband. But now I want honesty. It was you, not Heather, who was out with Hugh Jeffries that Saturday night. You have been identified as the woman who spent an evening with him at Bell's Hotel. Also as the woman who made a telephone call from a cottage in Long Lane at around the time you say you were with your sister on a car park in Glevebourne. Now I'd like the truth."

"There's nothing else I can tell you."

"For God's sake, woman, think! You heard me say back there that the Carlton was pushed—"

"All right, so you know!"

"Pushed, Mrs. Abbott—by someone attempting to conceal a murder."

"Not murder, Mr. Bassett. Hugh died of car injuries."

"I'm sorry," Bassett said. "It hasn't been released to the media yet, but Hugh was definitely murdered."

She turned to look at him. "You wouldn't lie—?"

"Not about something like that, no."

"How—?"

"I'm afraid I can't tell you that. All I can tell you is that Hugh did not die from his car injuries."

No histrionics. No tears; nor even a moan. Alison Abbott had her emotions well under control. As Bassett had anticipated. "I'm trying to fathom . . ." she began. "I can't see . . . Hugh was all right when—when—"

"When you left him?" Bassett said quietly.

"Yes. When I left him," she said, barely audibly.

She looked at Bassett again. "When did it happen?"

"Hugh was alone for ten minutes while your sister and her husband were hooking the Carlton onto the breakdown vehicle. When they went to the cottage afterwards to collect Hugh, he was dead."

"Someone went in—?" She shuddered. "The gipsies?" And when Bassett did not reply: "You think it was me?"

"Could have been," Bassett said forthrightly. "You could have driven off, turned around, and come in from the bottom end of Long Lane, to sit and await your chance—"

"I assure you I didn't. Why would I want to kill Hugh?"

"You've just told me you love your husband, want to save him from being hurt. I suspect—forgive me if I'm wrong—that you didn't always love him, that Jeffries had prime claim on your affections. If Hugh wouldn't let you go, or threatened to go to your husband—there's a motive."

"Hugh would never have done such a thing. He was a good man." She seemed to start a sigh, stifle it. "You are right about one thing, though. Almost right. That was to have been the last time I saw Hugh. We had said our goodbyes. I'd fallen in love with my husband—it was as simple as that. Hugh and I had one last meal together, and Hugh was taking me to my car, only calling at Crum Cottage for a bottle of whisky. He'd not be going there again, he said, he wasn't going to leave the whisky there to go bad. His little joke."

She pulled her coat around her. It wasn't cold, but she had started shivering, reaction setting in.

"Right, Mr. Bassett," she said, no-nonsense fashion. "I'll do what has to be done. Do I have to go with you?"

"Not yet," Bassett said. "Tell me about that night."

"The Saturday? It's as Heather and Nigel said. We hit a tree, I rang them up, Heather came out, we got Hugh to the cottage . . ."

In short, Heather Davis had spoken the truth.

"I don't know why I went along with the insurance claim," she continued. "I think I was numbed, I know that I lost several days; and I've never been able to recall that Christmas clearly . . . They told me Hugh was dead, that their plan was foolproof; as long as there was an accident *some*where to account for the condition of the Carlton . . . When two days passed and there was nothing on the news I thought they must have been mistaken, that Hugh had come round, was in hospital and couldn't let me know. Heather lived in hopes too . . . And then came the news of Hugh's disappearance. I wanted to tell the police where he was. I wanted to tell David everything. But I couldn't do it, it was too late . . . If I'd done the decent thing then for Hugh, I'd have implicated Heather and Nigel, which would have been unfair after they had done so much for me. The real truth was, it would have taken a heap of guts to own up. I hadn't the guts, quite frankly . . . I was stuck in a vicious circle."

She sighed. "I shouldn't have left Hugh, should I? I thought he'd be all right with Heather. I thought she'd stay with him; Nigel could have attended to the Carlton on his own. But I can understand why Hugh sent her from him. Poor Heather, Hugh couldn't stand the sight of her . . . I suppose she rabbited on at him with that silly voice she puts on sometimes, babying him because he was ill. She can get on your nerves after a while . . ." She gave a nervous little laugh. "Now I'm rabbiting on."

From somewhere close by came a short excited bark. Alison stood up. "The dogs out for their bedtime romp. We usually all go together."

"Then what are you waiting for?" Bassett gave her a gentle push. "Go on," he urged as they began walking to the front of the house. "I'll phone you later. Confide in your husband. It may not be as bad as you think. You may find he already knows —or has a very good idea. Go."

He passed them shortly afterwards as he drove down the drive. They were walking side by side. Abbott's arm was round Alison's shoulders.

Bassett drove on a mile, stopped, got out of his car, and walked under the stars, smoking a thinking pipe. He felt variously sad, angry, disturbed. When he had puffed his last plume of smoke he looked at his watch. He had a final call to make. And then . . .

There was a light on at the back of Davis's Garage. No sign of activity, but worth a look, Bassett thought.

He was right. Light trickled thinly from the door of a workshop at the rear. Someone was in there. Bassett made a noise as he approached the entrance, scuffing his feet and calling softly, "That you, Stan?" so as not to scare the pants off whoever it was.

"In here!" Stan was rolling a lorry wheel into a safety cage; showed no great surprise when he looked up and saw Bassett. "Won't be a sec. Bloke wants this for first thing in the morning." A puncture; repaired; only needed air now. Bassett watched him inflate the tyre, looked to see which hand he used the most.

"Nigel and Heather haven't come back yet." Stan somehow managed to make it a question.

"No," Bassett replied. "They're still at the station." A pause. "You've known Heather a long time."

"We go back a long way." The benevolent face turned wooden momentarily; then came a smile. "Sweethearts when we were six. Got a walloping from my ma for pinching her best lace handkerchief to give to my ladylove. Daintiest thing I could find."

"I gave my first sweetheart a box of paints," Bassett said. "Cost sixpence, I think, from Woolworth's."

They grinned at each other. Stan tossed Bassett a clean rag and pointed. Bassett spread the rag and sat on the upturned oil drum.

"There. Done." Stan screwed the tyre's valve cap on, wound the hose round a wheel on the wall, switched off the compressor, wiped his hands on a rag, and checked the time. "He might collect it tonight. I'll give him half an hour. If he's not here by eleven I'll call it a day." He took out his cigarettes. "Smoke?"

"Pipe." Bassett patted his pocket. "Not long put one out . . . Do you often work late?"

"In emergencies."

"What do you do—take it in turns?"

"We work it out between us. The mechanics, Nigel and myself. It's flexible," Stan said, blowing out his match.

"Explain something for me, please," Bassett said. "That Saturday night—you know the one I mean now—Mr. Davis says he received an emergency call, chap run out of juice. He and Mrs. Davis had been out for the evening. I imagine they had a few drinks. I'd have thought someone else would have been on call that night."

Stan pulled up another oil drum. "Nigel would have been safe enough. He sticks religiously to non-alcoholic drinks when he's driving. But it's true, we're normally better organized. It was Nigel's weekend on call, matter of fact, but this function came up, a last-minute thing, and I offered to stand in for him. Until he got home, was the agreement. And it's always the way," he said philosophically; "not a peep out of the phone all night, but no sooner had I put the phones through than the calls start. I was taking the dog for a walk a few minutes later when I saw Nigel take off up the road in the Land-Rover. I felt a mite awkward about it, to be honest, thought he would think I'd been a bit quick off the mark."

Bassett chose his next words with care. "Mrs. Davis says she went out shortly afterwards. She says you could have seen her leave."

Stan looked.

"Perhaps you would confirm her story," Bassett said.

"What has she told you?"

"Ah." Bassett smiled. "That's not how we do it."

"No, I suppose not. All right. I did see Heather go out. I'd decided to wait up, and when Nigel got back I was going to take over the phone again. About five minutes later I heard a car. Looked out of the window—Heather. I thought Nigel'd had to ask her to run out with whatever he was short of. Felt a bit rotten about that."

"So you went after her," Bassett said.

"I thought it might be a two-man breakdown. So I got my car out, yes." Stan studied the last inch of his cigarette before stubbing it out underfoot. "I was going to flag her down, but I got this feeling that I might be poking my nose. Thinking about it, there hadn't been time for Nigel to reach a breakdown, diagnose the trouble, find out he wasn't carrying the parts he needed, and get Heather. I didn't know it was a petrol call, of course. She hadn't called at the garage to pick anything up. Nothing was coming over the radio, no directions or anything. And she seemed to know exactly where she was going."

"But you didn't turn back."

"Not then, no." Stan seemed reluctant to continue. "I know about Long Lane," Bassett said. "I can describe what Heather was wearing . . ."

"Her white coat."

"Yes. We know the whole story. But it helps if we have verification."

"All right. If you know . . . I stayed with it," Stan said. "Followed Heather to Long Lane. Saw her brake lights go on by a cottage. She didn't stop there, so I guessed she wanted the next one up. I pulled onto the next stretch of grass and followed on foot. Heard voices, saw what looked like a parked car, couldn't really see all that much, but it sounded as if there were

two or three people there, so I went back to my car for a smoke
. . . I suppose I *was* poking my nose from then on. Wanted to
know what was going on.

"There was some movement: one, maybe two people went
with Heather to the cottage. I recognized her by the coat, didn't
recognize anybody else, they were only shapes . . . A few
minutes went by. Heather and another person left the cottage.
And then I heard her on the radio. Talking to Nigel. I got out of
my car, began walking again—but I heard Heather's car drive
off—"

"You heard it? It didn't pass you?"

"No, it must have carried on up. Funny thing was, though—"

"Are you there, Stan?" They both looked towards the workshop entrance as footsteps sounded outside. The man for the
tyre. A hulk of a man dressed in cowboy shirt and jeans. "Glad
I'm not the only one keeping you up!" he said in a bluff friendly
manner. "I can wait," he told Stan. "If there's a hold-up . . ."

"No, no, it's ready for you . . ."

Bassett filled his pipe.

"Where was I?" Stan asked, after the man had gone.

"We were talking about Heather's car," Bassett said. "You
were saying it was a funny thing . . ."

TWENTY-SEVEN

At ten o'clock the following morning the interview room in
Glevebourne Police Station was looking crowded. Nigel and
Heather Davis were there; Alison and David Abbott; and Stan
Harding. They had been invited by Inspector Bob Greenaway
at Bassett's request. Bassett was the last to arrive: from the
direction of the canteen, bulging carrier-bag, handle stretched
to breaking point, in one hand, hat in the other.

Bob Greenaway was waiting for him outside the door.
"You're late."

Bassett winked: no humour in it. "Edgy, are they?"

"I thought you said nine-thirty."

"Got meself lost," Bassett said blandly. "Better get in there before they start stamping their feet."

Bob preceded him, joining Sergeant Miller, already there. Bassett counted to ten, then made an entrance.

"Sorry to keep you waiting, everybody. Lost track of time doing me shopping." With scarcely a glance at his audience Bassett heaved the bag onto the table, and dropped his hat next to it. "Something in here to show you. Bear with me if you will while I find it."

He began rummaging in the bag. One of those looking thought he was a buffoon. So, a buffoon he would be.

"Cabbage. Ten bob that cost me!" He placed the cabbage on the table, steadied it so that it wouldn't roll. "Shocking! Used to be sixpence this time of year!"

Feet shuffled.

"Ah! now this was a bargain"—bringing out a big marrow-bone wrapped in butcher's cling film—"only cost me ten pee." Triumphantly.

"Anyhow. You all know by now what I mean when I say the night Hugh Jeffries died . . ."

He looked at nobody in particular. In fact, he might have been emptying groceries onto his kitchen table for all the real attention he paid anybody.

"On that night the Judge had taken an old friend, Mrs. Abbott, out for a meal. They were returning to town via Long Lane. Unfortunately he was driving a car he was not too familiar with, took a bend too fast, and hit a tree. Mrs. Abbott went to the house of friends of mine, rang up her sister, Mrs. Davis, and Mrs. Davis came out to help. Together the two women got the injured Mr. Jeffries to the cottage, made him as comfortable as possible, then they both returned to Mrs. Davis's car, from where Mrs. Davis radioed her husband . . . He was already out on an emergency call as it happened, so wasn't too far away

. . . Mrs. Davis then gave the keys of her car to Mrs. Abbott and Mrs. Abbott drove off . . ."

Packet soups, Oxos, garlic had joined other items on the table.

"Mrs. Davis returned to the cottage. She was concerned for Hugh Jeffries, thought an ambulance ought to have been called, but apparently Mr. Jeffries had expressly asked for this to be deferred. He proposed eventually to go to a private clinic to be patched up . . . Mrs. Davis stayed only a few minutes, she says, before going back to the Carlton to wait for her husband . . . Mr. Davis duly arrived, he and his wife hooked up the Carlton, drove on to the cottage—Mr. Davis went in— and found Mr. Jeffries dead.

"Most, if not all of you, thought I was investigating insurance fraud. I never was. What I was investigating was murder. Hugh Jeffries didn't die of injuries received in the car accident. The man was murdered."

Cheese, baked beans, a can of fruit juice . . .

"And not without premeditation," Bassett continued. "Hugh wasn't killed in the heat of a single moment with the first weapon to hand: his killer had time to plan and wax cunning. Time to decide *not* to strike the killing blow. A sneaky blow, Hugh unsuspecting, probably sitting with his head back, eyes closed. It wouldn't have mattered if he had opened them. He knew his killer, wouldn't have been afraid—until perhaps that very last second. The killer tiptoed in, no doubt assuming solicitude—and struck. Here. On the forehead. On a spot already marked by its contact with the car windscreen."

"It's horrible." A low horrified murmur from Heather.

"As you say, Mrs. Davis: horrible. Murder is. If anyone wishes to say more we could talk in private."

Silence.

"No?" Bassett said. "Very well." He had come to the final item in the carrier-bag. Something heavy. Something Bassett handled almost reverently. Something not unlike a pudding wrapped in a white cloth . . . As Bassett put the bundle on the table he flicked an eye, glimpsed a variety of expressions, including the one he sought; then he began methodically to re-pack the carrier-bag.

"Who might have done it?" Bassett said. "Gipsies? Wasn't there something about gipsies and a threat? But how could they have known where the Judge was going to be at any particular time? They would have had to see him in the Carlton, would virtually have had to track him for the remainder of the day; and so on and so on—missing a score of opportunities. Plus the best of them all—when Mr. Jeffries was in the wrecked car and Mrs. Abbott was at a nearby house making that telephone call.

"Who then? Mr. Davis? He could have done it when he went to fetch Mr. Jeffries. We only have his word for it that Hugh was *already* dead.

"But what would have been his motive? And when did he think of it? If he *was* the killer, I tell myself, he must have thought of it either after receiving his wife's radio message *or* upon arrival and her embarking on the tale . . . It would have been the *accident* that put the idea into his head, so surely he would have used the *accident* to cover the murder. He wouldn't have shifted the Carlton—he'd have bunged the body back in the car and left the accident to be discovered—with luck, in the morning. To all intents and purposes Hugh would have died at the wheel.

"There was, I understand, Mrs. Abbott to consider. There was that telephone call she made. And what if the breakdown truck had been heard—or seen—going by? No problem! Mrs. Abbott's Volvo had broken down! It would've been there in the garage for the police to see . . . And Mr. Davis would have been in a far happier position than the one in which he actually found himself. For one thing, he wouldn't have had to mess with that fake accident . . . He panicked, he said, when he found the Judge was dead. He panicked and ran. I believe him.

"Mr. Abbott might have had a motive for the murder. But Mr. Abbott was absent from home that weekend. It turns out that he was delivering Christmas parcels to relatives in various parts of the Midlands, so unfortunately eighteen months on he has no alibi. For whom among those relatives would be able to recall *accurately* the time Mr. Abbott left one house and arrived at the next? . . . He could have nipped home on the motor-way.

"But I don't think so. Mr. Abbott didn't have to kill Hugh Jeffries to get rid of him. Jeffries was a judge: a threat of disclosure would have done the trick.

"Who do we have left? Mrs. Abbott. Mrs. Davis. I tell myself that if Mrs. Abbott had wanted to kill Hugh she could have done it while he was in the Carlton. No telephone call. No allowing herself to be seen. Disappear into the night, and no one the wiser. Again—to all intents and purposes the man would have died at the wheel.

"On the other hand, Mrs. Abbott *did* play a part in the fake accident business. She must have had a darned good reason for doing so. Only in retrospect was it completely foolproof: at the time no one could be certain it wouldn't go wrong. So—"

There was an interruption. "For God's sake, man! It's crystal clear that whoever killed Jeffries did it while he was alone in the cottage!" David Abbott's voice was strident. "While Nigel and Heather were hooking up the Carlton. My wife had already left—"

Bassett shook his head. "I did say, Mr. Abbott, that the killer had a short time to think about it. Your wife drove away, yes; but she could have come back, could have come in from the bottom end of the lane—and killed Hugh Jeffries as an *after-thought.*"

"No!" The cry came from Heather Davis.

Only now, his shopping-bag refilled and standing on the floor, did Bassett look directly at his audience. A slow, sweeping look. Which rested longest on Stan Harding's bowed head. And finally moved to Heather.

"You're quite right, Mrs. Davis; Alison didn't return via the bottom end of the lane. There was someone there. If Mrs.

Abbott or anyone else had been in the bottom lane that night he or she would have been seen.

"But the few minutes that you and Mr. Davis were working on the Carlton wasn't the only time Hugh Jeffries was alone. There was another time. He was alone while you and your sister went to the car to use your radio—"

Bassett opened out the pudding cloth, exposing a lump of rock to view.

"—*alone until you went back to comfort him.*"

Bassett hated himself for what that did to the lovely face. She was stunned. Looked pole-axed.

He looked away: at Alison Abbott.

"I didn't do it." The little-girl voice. Pleading. "I didn't kill Hugh, I swear."

She wasn't telling Bassett this, she was looking at her husband, beseeching him to believe her. He did, and he told Bassett so, adding heatedly, "Heather hasn't seen the man in years!"

"Which may well be the reason for killing him," said Bassett. "Do you remember, Mrs. Davis? I asked you over and over again if you knew your sister was seeing Hugh, if you knew about the cottage. You insisted you knew nothing. I watched you. You were speaking the truth; you did not know. Wasn't that what infuriated you? The *deceit?* They had been seeing each other for a couple of years, had the gall even to hire cars from your husband, Hugh for anonymity, Alison for the excuse she could make if she was ever spotted by someone who knew her. But flaunting it, if you had guessed. And if you hadn't, they had been laughing behind your back. You didn't know—and you were furious when you did find out, that night.

"I thought it strange that Mrs. Abbott left so easily when you said—reiterated—how ill Hugh was, and in pain. *Of course* you went on about Hugh being worse than he was admitting to . . . *Of course* you were agitated when your husband arrived . . .

You had to get the point home. You wanted him not to be taken utterly aback when he found Hugh dead.''

"No! He was ill. I swear it.''

"Weren't you applying the same tactic when you came to me to volunteer what had happened? Didn't you say to yourself: he's getting to be a nuisance, if he keeps on digging he'll find out we all knew Hugh? And didn't you say to yourself: if I let him know about the car crash—and how Hugh died of his injuries—they might let it go at that? Isn't that why you volunteered? . . . For eighteen months you had committed a perfect murder. It might have become the perfect murder; it was pure chance the body was discovered. Hugh could have been there for years.''

"No, no, no. *No.* He *was* ill. I haven't lied. I've told the truth, I swear,'' she entreated.

"But surely''—Bassett softened his tone—"if he had been as ill as you say, Alison would have stayed. She wouldn't have put self-preservation first—''

He broke off, sent a look towards the Abbotts, saw the expression on David Abbott's face, addressed Alison. "*Would* you, Mrs. Abbott?'' He barked it. "You'd have taken him in Heather's car to a doctor. Or fetched a doctor. You didn't. You drove off alone. I wonder why.''

He turned again to Heather Davis. "Where did you get the mud on your car?''

"I never have a dirty car.'' She glanced at Stan.

"That evening you and your husband went out in your car. Where did you get the mud? There was mud on your car.'' He spoke very softly now. She was hot and bothered and looked extremely tired.

"Nowhere. We only had to travel two miles.''

"Main road all the way? And when you drove out to your sister you stuck to roads—you took no short cuts along muddy tracks?''

"I didn't know any short cuts—I—''

"Mrs. Abbott!" Again Bassett barked. "Why did you hose down Heather's car on the Sunday morning?"

The only response was her chair creaking.

David Abbott was strangely quiet.

"Why, why, why? So many whys, Mrs. Abbott. Why that nonsense about any questions asked, your car had broken down, you borrowed Heather's? Questions asked by whom? Your husband was away, you are the lady of the house, what you do with your car is nobody's business but your own. Why the build-up of secrecy? Yes, build-up. Was it *really* so important, once you realized Hugh was injured? Why the desperate rush to get away—while half-pretending quite the opposite? A mild form of brainwashing, wasn't it? Directed at Heather. So that when—for her—the unexpected did happen she would remember that secrecy was to be observed. The story was planted in her mind: Alison's car broke down, I lent her mine. Perhaps you hoped Nigel would put the body back in the car . . .

"Or perhaps you didn't think that far ahead. Your plan to kill Hugh took up every space in your head. You didn't think of killing him till you got back from making that telephone call and saw him still in the Carlton. Was that when it occurred to you: perhaps he'll die . . . Perhaps you wished him dead. Perhaps that was when the seed was sown . . . Dead. Dead. If only he were dead . . .

"Too late! You had rung up Heather; she was on her way . . . When you made that call it was simply for Heather to fetch you, to take you back to your own car; then Hugh would have dealt with the accident. You thought perhaps he was a walking casualty. And then you realized he was not. He was worse than you had thought. Your sister recognized the fact immediately. But not ill enough to die without help . . ."

A silence of only seconds, but a silence which had lasted long enough.

"Why did you hose the car down?" Bassett repeated. "I'll tell you why. Because you *did* go back to Hugh, only not by the bottom lane. You drove round to the back tracks. You wouldn't have collected mud on the car that night if you had kept to the road; it was a frosty night. There was only one way you could have got the car muddy—that was by driving *through* mud . . .

"You heard Heather make the radio call, heard her ask Nigel if he needed Stan or another mechanic . . . And you heard Nigel's reply—that at a pinch he could manage on his own, but if Heather would be there, just in case. You knew, therefore, that Hugh would be alone for some minutes.

"You drove off, returned via the back tracks, picked up a rock in the back garden, waited until you heard the Land-Rover, and then you took the rock and tiptoed in to Hugh . . .

"You had already noticed that any movement near his chair cast huge shadows on the wall as a result of there being only a flashlamp for light. No one looking in would see you strike the blow—but they might see the shadow. Heather *might* come back again; Nigel *might* come to take a look at Hugh before dealing with the Carlton. So you pulled that one curtain across . . ."

Bassett paused; then, "Remember I said there was a watcher in the lane?" He left the rest to imagination.

A heavier silence fell.

Should he go on? Should he say: There wasn't *time* to close both sets of curtains, there wasn't time to check for anything left behind on previous visits, there wasn't time for anything but to strike that blow.

He glimpsed David Abbott, felt sorry for the man. How much had she told him last night? A little—or nothing at all? The expression on Abbott's face earlier, when he was accusing Heather, and he, Bassett, had told the man about Hugh Jeffries and his wife . . . Abbott might have suspected, but he hadn't *known*.

Bassett said quietly, "Shall I go on, Mrs. Abbott? Shall I explain why you killed Hugh Jeffries?"

David Abbott intervened. "Alison will tell us herself." He spoke as quietly as Bassett. He had been sitting with legs folded, elbow on knee, face covered by an outspread hand.

Now he rubbed at his forehead, as if to massage away a head-ache. "Bring the thing to an end, if you will, please, Alison."

"I can't say why anything. I don't know . . ."

"Don't be a fool." It was astonishingly calm. "Do you think I don't know you were seeing him? Do you think I haven't had nightmares ever since I heard he had gone missing? Which of you wanted to finish—?"

"Oh, David! How can you ask that!" Alison reproached. "I wanted to finish it. Hugh wanted me to get a divorce. I wouldn't. It was you I loved all alone, and I'd been too stupid to realize it . . ." She seemed little girl all of a sudden, might almost have been imitating Heather. "We had a row. Hugh was going to tell you everything, so that *you* would divorce *me*. He wouldn't listen to reason. He was going to tell you everything. I couldn't let that happen, I couldn't bear for you to be hurt . . . Truly, David, truly I love you . . ."

Bassett looked at Bob Greenaway, picked up the rock and his shopping-bag, and left the room.

TWENTY-EIGHT

Stan Harding caught up with Bassett in the corridor. Bassett turned to speak to him. "I'm sorry I had to put you through that, Mr. Harding. I didn't know how it would go. I might have had to ask you a question or two."

The other nodded. "It's all right. I'm sorry any of us had to come." He hesitated, smiled a weary smile. "I was beginning to sweat at one point. I thought you had me taped for it."

"I knew you hadn't done it," Bassett said. "The blow was struck by a right-handed person." He motioned towards Stan's right hand. A physical impossibility. "You could not have held the rock." No grip in the palm.

Stan felt in his pocket for cigarettes. "Heather . . . I

thought you had misunderstood me last night. I—" He shook his head, a frown not far away. "She had no cause."

"None whatsoever," Bassett said.

"I didn't see Alison close those curtains," Stan said awkwardly.

Bassett smiled. "I never said you did. I simply reminded Alison that there had been a watcher. I didn't say for how long."

They looked at each other in silence for a moment. Stan was the first to look away. "How did you know I was there? I thought—last night—when we were talking—" He lit a cigarette. "I thought Heather had seen me."

"No," Bassett said. "Heather didn't see you. And I didn't know you were there. I thought it was odd for Mr. Davis to be called out after an evening out on the tiles. It crossed my mind that if he took the emergency because the one actually on call— you, perhaps—was already out, you might have picked up the radio message." Might have known more than you were telling, he could have added.

"Queer do," Stan said. He said it to himself as he left. No goodbye. Just a kind of salute.

There was much Bassett would have liked to ask Stan: about exactly how much he *had* seen that night, or later had guessed, but it would only have been to satisfy his own curiosity. He let the man go. Dragged his feet a little to let him get ahead.

He hadn't hung around for long after he listened in to Heather's radio call, Stan had said last night when they resumed their conversation following the tyre man's departure. He had been in two minds about what to do. A breakdown which Nigel said he could handle himself—should he stay and offer assistance, or not? He was debating with himself when he saw Heather, her white coat, coming down the lane again—and suddenly he realized how long he had been there. If he showed himself now they would wonder what he was up to . . . He dared not leave by carrying on up the lane—Nigel would be arriving from that direction—so he reversed down the way he had come. Which took a little time. And then he stopped for a smoke. It was then that he thought he saw Heather's car leaving from a track at the bottom end.

"Funny thing," he had said. "I couldn't figure out how it got there . . ."

And Bassett had remembered Jill Martin saying something about Alison hosing down the car on the Sunday.

After that, last night, those other questions hadn't mattered. Nor did they now. Let the man go. Let him go.

"Which of them was it?" the desk sergeant inquired when Bassett stopped to pass the time of day. "Not Heather Davis?"

Bassett grinned. You too? "No, not Heather Davis," he said.

He had once half-suspected her. She was, in the kindest meaning of the word, simple-minded, and the simple-minded can be cunning. She might have lied and twisted everything, as Alison had suggested. And have volunteered to come clean about the circumstances of Hugh's death for the reason he had just now given. The very fact that the full story was so obviously rehearsed was itself vaguely suspect . . . But when it came down to feasibility it had to be Alison who killed Hugh. When it came to feasibility Alison was the only one with a real motive. Alison had a powerful motive.

He said cheerio to the desk sergeant, descended the steps, and crossed the station car park to the flowerbed. He found the spot, put the rock back where he had taken it from.

It wasn't *the* rock. It had only been a prop. Alison was aware of it. All the same, it had served its purpose: it had let Alison know.

She had more or less confessed to her guilt as far as Bassett was concerned when she told him, quote, "I'd fallen in love with my husband." He had been able to imagine what had happened. She had loved Hugh Jeffries. He was perhaps the first man who ever told her she was beautiful, the first to appreciate her as a woman, the first to make her feel good. In theory she would love him for the rest of their lives, whether or not they married. But—Bassett, the romantic, reasoned—she wasn't *in love* with him, and that made the difference. When David Abbott came on the scene she chose him. He had more to offer. She did marry Abbott for his wealth and lifestyle. It was just possible that her sister's affair with Hugh Jeffries had nothing to do with it, possible, indeed likely, that Hugh was comforted by Heather after he discovered that Alison had another man in her life. Possible that Hugh always loved Alison more than she had ever loved him.

When all was revealed, Alison might well say she had begun seeing Hugh again more out of pity or remorse than anything else. Only if she were honest would she say she wanted to eat her cake and have it. An affair with Hugh was fine, so long as her husband never found out, and so long as Hugh accepted that it was an affair, nothing more.

When Hugh became too serious, when she realized she *was in love* with her husband, and that Hugh might ruin everything . . . and the opportunity arose to get rid of Hugh forever . . . she took it.

She had decided long ago that never again would anyone take what she wanted away from her. She wanted David. She wanted to keep him.

Bassett went home.

Home. Be it ever so humble . . . Bassett the all-wise, the all-powerful, he from whom all bounty flowed, would be treated to such a welcome by his birds and animals! But there was no one to ask now: are you tired? Hungry? Cold? What kind of day have you had? There were days when he missed Mary terribly.

This was one of those days. He wanted her to be at home today. He wanted to wrap his arms around her, feel her softness, hear her voice, have her listen to what he had to say about the case . . . Instead, he talked to his hens, and Cocky, and pup. Why not? They liked to hear his voice. It was soothing, warm, gave them a sense of security.

In due course, Jack the Poacher would hear from Rosie-from-Hereford's son in Australia. The Brother would tell Jack he had no knowledge of the alleged theft by and ensuing conviction of Aaron and Isaac Smith; his mother's solicitors had informed him only of the contents of the will. But in the letter—yes, yes, it was here!—his mother made it clear that she was going to give Great-Grandmother Adeline's porcelain to Aaron and Ike.

That letter would subsequently lead to a re-opening of the case.

Tod Arkwright never would get those honesty seedheads for his daughter. When he went to look, the plant had vanished. There were those who would say the plant had never existed. Tod, of course, knew better. Belatedly, the teller of tall tales would recollect that Tabitha had been credited by some with having the Eye . . . 'Tweren't no bird dropped the seed 'tween those paving stones, he would say, it were Tabitha's doing . . . Tabitha had reckoned the Judge had been sitting in her cottage long enough. All she had wanted was for the plant to thrive long enough to catch Tod's attention.

Daniel Smith would attribute the honesty plant to Fleur. Fleur wanted Aaron and Ike to be free.

Jack the Poacher, when forced to give an opinion, would say with a twinkle in his eye that it was probably six of Tabitha and half a dozen of Fleur—a means of settling their differences.

Bassett? He would say nothing. He would remember the day police swarmed over Crum Cottage; and size fourteens never leave a blade of grass unsquashed.

But all that was in the future. Today Bassett began building a house of straw in his orchard, a summer house for his two new piglets, the pair of Old Spot weaners who had chosen him at market. Jack had taken the weaners to his place, housing them in a loose-box until Bassett would be free to give them his undivided care. Well, that was now.

"Jack—?" he said on the telephone that evening. "About Pinky and Perky. Eh . . . ? Yes, all over . . . Yes, it was . . . Yes, a great pity, I agree."

A very great pity. He had liked the lady. He'd liked her very much.

ABOUT THE AUTHOR

Pat Burden was born in Birmingham, England. Educated at Stafford Girls' High School, she has been a nurse, a secretary, has worked in public relations, and for British Rail and a national bus company. She loves to travel, and in the sixties took off with her husband, Land-Rover, and tent overland in Australia, where among other adventures she cleared virgin bush with axe, machete, and rope, and sweated in a laundry in subtropical Queensland.

She now lives in an isolated cottage in Herefordshire, England, with her husband and their beautiful Labrador, and when not writing enjoys reading, cooking, embroidery, and walking.